THE DOCTOR'S DILEMMA

THE DOCTOR'S DILEMMA

•

Victoria M. Johnson

AVALON BOOKS
NEW YORK

*This book is for all the medics who served in the
Air Force with my husband and I; and for the doctors,
nurses, and medical professionals who cared for
my dear mom when she needed it most; and in
memory of my much-loved brothers who are
now in heaven with Mom. And to my husband,
Michael, who still makes my heart go pitter-patter.*

Published by Avalon Books,
an imprint of Thomas Bouregy & Co., Inc.
160 Madison Avenue, New York, NY 10016

Library of Congress Cataloging-in-Publication Data

Johnson, Victoria M.
  The doctor's dilemma / Victoria Johnson.
      p. cm.
  ISBN 978-0-8034-7670-7
  1. Clinics—Mexico—Fiction.   2. Americans—Mexico—
Fiction.   3. Physicians—Fiction.   4. Nurse and physician—
Fiction.   I. Title.
  PS3610.O38365D63 2011
  813'.6—dc22

                                                          2011005557

PRINTED IN THE UNITED STATES OF AMERICA
ON ACID-FREE PAPER
BY RR DONNELLEY, BLOOMSBURG, PENNSYLVANIA

Chapter One

Dr. Ryan Novak glanced at the wide-open door of his clinic and the small crowd gathered on the porch, and he knew something was wrong. He hurried up the dirt path as fast as he could in his dripping wet swim trunks and flip-flops.

"Apurate!" The throng of Mexican villagers shouted at him to hurry.

"Qué pasa?" What's happening? he asked as he rushed past the threshold and into the clinic.

An eleven-year-old local boy named Jaime cried loudly, covered in angry cuts and bruises. His mother and siblings hovered over him, trying to calm him, while an unfamiliar, dark-haired beauty tending to the boy shouted orders in English to Father Sanchez, the local priest.

Father Sanchez bolted toward the supply closet.

Ryan gently made his way through the huddle, silently praying, *Please don't let that woman be the nurse the agency sent.*

1

Father Sanchez emerged and deposited supplies at the woman's side. Then he spotted Ryan. "Doctor!"

The woman glanced up from irrigating the boy's wounds, and her dark brown eyes widened as her gaze skimmed over Ryan from head to foot. He thought he heard her gasp.

"He fell off the roof of his house onto an old rotary lawn mower. In addition to his lacerations I think he has broken his arm," she said.

Ryan leaned over the boy. "Jaime, I'm here," he said.

Jaime calmed down a bit but continued crying.

"Did he hit his head? Lose consciousness?" Ryan asked while assessing the boy's wounds. From what he could see of Jaime's face and chest and shredded, blood-soaked shirt and pants, Ryan knew he'd need dozens of sutures.

"His pupils are evenly dilated and responsive," the dark-haired woman said as she continued to pour saline solution onto gauze pads and efficiently dab the child's lacerations. "His mother told me that his brothers witnessed the fall, and he never lost consciousness."

"You speak Spanish?" he asked.

"Yes. Of course."

Ryan frowned at the villagers. "Everybody, out. Jaime'll be fine." His voice softened as he spoke to the boy's young brothers and sisters. "You too. Wait outside."

Father Sanchez guided everyone out and closed the door.

"Neuro check?" Ryan slipped his hands under the boy's body and palpated along his spinal column.

"Positive responses to stimuli. His left arm appears to be broken," she said.

He examined the arm. "It's a closed reduction fracture,"

he agreed. He looked into the boy's eyes. "Jaime, close your eyes and stick out your tongue," he said.

The boy complied.

"Okay, stop. You look silly," he teased, pleased, though, that the child could perform both tasks at the same time.

"Am I going to die?" Jaime asked bravely.

"No, son. I'm taking you into an exam room, and we'll fix you like new." Ryan lifted the boy and carried him into one of the clinic's two examination rooms. He walked carefully in the flip-flops, and Jaime's mother, Father Sanchez, and the dark-haired beauty followed his trail of seawater drops.

"Please have a seat in the waiting room," he said in Spanish to the boy's mother.

"I will wait with her," Father Sanchez said. "But first let me introduce you two."

Ryan had a bad feeling in his gut. Maybe the unfamiliar woman wasn't his nurse. Maybe she was a tourist who'd happened upon the scene at the clinic.

"Dr. Ryan Novak, please welcome Nurse Grace Sinclair."

Silence filled the room as Ryan inwardly groaned. This *couldn't* be the nurse the agency had hired. They'd said she was a mature widow. This woman couldn't be any older than twenty-six.

Neither of them smiled, and neither offered a hand to shake.

"With all the commotion, I neglected to introduce myself," she said.

"Nurse Sinclair," Ryan said tersely.

"Please call me Grace." She glanced at Father Sanchez with a bewildered expression.

Ryan knew the reason behind her confusion, but his explanation could wait. "Welcome to La Clínica Pediátrica. Let's get to work."

Father Sanchez said a prayer over the child and quietly departed.

Grace Sinclair had already begun to undress the boy, gently cutting through the torn clothing with scissors. "Will you use EMLA Cream to numb him?" she asked Ryan as Jaime winced and squirmed.

Without the bloody clothes Ryan could more clearly observe the extent of the injuries. "No, he's in too much pain. Start an IV with D5W." He turned to the little boy. "Jaime, I'm going to medicate you but keep you awake. Nurse Grace will put your arm in a sling for now, okay?"

The child nodded, and Ryan quickly retrieved morphine from a cabinet, grabbed the syringe and needle that Grace had set on the tray, and injected three milligrams into the IV.

"I wish I had an external fixator splint," Ryan said as he took a soft sling from a cabinet, "but this will have to do."

Grace smiled reassuringly at Jaime as she gently maneuvered his arm into the sling. Then she pulled the surgical light into position over the exam table.

"Give me a second to put on scrubs," Ryan said, wanting to get out of the trunks and flip-flops for the long procedure ahead.

"Do you have some for me?" Grace asked.

He nodded indifferently at the cabinet with linens and scrubs. But something inside him pulsated at the thought of her wearing his things. "Be right back, Jaime."

Ryan stepped into the room next door. Cursing under

his breath, he kicked off the flip-flops and tugged off his damp trunks. *Damn that agency.* He hastily pulled on scrubs and work shoes. She'd better be a qualified nurse, or he'd sue them. Of course she *had* handled the emergency until he'd arrived. Regardless, he would watch her closely over the next few hours. If she faltered, she would be out the door, and the agency would have hell to pay.

Hearing drawers opening and closing, he returned to the exam room. Grace had everything laid out on the tray—dissolvable sutures, Steri Strips, clamps. On a second tray she had Betadine poured into a sterile bowl, sterile cotton balls, gauze pads, more sutures, and clamps. She wore gloves and a pair of his scrubs. The top was too baggy on her, and she'd rolled up the pants. But she looked stunningly beautiful.

She's a grieving widow, for heaven's sake! Get a grip, Novak.

He scrubbed in, grabbing one of the sterile towels she'd set beside the sink. He donned surgical gloves and sat on the stool.

Grace kept busy. Throughout the procedure she tried anticipating Dr. Novak's needs and attempted to at least keep pace with him. As he tied off one suture, she used a clamp to pass him another one.

"The agency said you didn't have much pediatric experience," he said. *But not many nurses who did would be willing to relocate to a tiny Mexican village,* he reflected.

"I did an emergency-room rotation. Some patients were children. I learn fast, though."

He glanced at her, and Grace wondered what he was

thinking. She forced herself not to dwell on his looks, but that simple task challenged her. As his golden-brown hair dried, it curled appealingly. His skin smelled of the sea.

Slowly the odor of the antiseptic overpowered his scent. With that distraction gone, Grace kept her attention on Novak's hands. He tirelessly worked magic with his hands.

A doctor revealed a great deal about himself through his touch. Grace had observed many physicians over the four years she'd been a nurse. There were those who yanked and twisted and got the job done, and those, like Dr. Novak, who spoke to the patient and examined with a firm but heedful touch.

"Can you let his mom know we're almost done?" he asked her.

Grace nodded and tossed the cotton gauze pad she'd just used to wipe the doctor's brow. She felt as wilted as the pad, but she strode out of the examination room for the second time to reassure Jaime's mother. She liked the way Novak was showing compassion toward the worried family.

"Nurse, how is my son?" The boy's father had arrived.

"Dr. Novak's almost finished mending his injuries. Jaime's been so brave. They'll both be out soon."

"Thank you, *señorita*." The father translated for his wife.

"Call me Grace, please."

The parents rose and hugged her, surprising Grace.

Grace returned to the exam room. As she washed and slapped on fresh gloves, Dr. Novak applied the final sutures. Grace assisted with applying several Steri Strips. When they finished, the floor was strewn with wrappers from all the dressings they had had to use. "How many stitches? I counted a hundred and ten."

Removing his surgical mask, Novak grinned. "Close. Try one twenty-six."

Grace ignored the doctor's enticing smile.

"Jaime, I think that's a record for San Felipe."

"Really? You think I'll be famous?" the groggy child said.

"I think you're *already* famous for the most broken bones in all of Mexico." Dr. Novak sat the boy up. "Let's take care of that arm."

"Won't you X-ray it first?" Grace asked.

"The clinic doesn't have X-ray capability yet."

"Don't tell me it's not gonna hurt, because I know it will." Jaime closed his eyes tightly.

"When are you going to learn to stay off roofs?" Dr. Novak removed the temporary sling.

"I like to explore."

"Your dad has pigs to feed, palm trees to trim, and hay to bale. Why don't you explore as you're working?"

"I fell from the fence of the pigpen as I fed the animals, out of a palo tree as I pruned, and off the hayloft as I pitched hay."

Grace was pleased that Dr. Novak kept the boy occupied as he reexamined the fracture and prepared to set the bone.

"And what were you doing on the roof? Sweeping?"

As Jaime opened his mouth to protest, Novak made his move. An ugly cracking sound filled the room. Jaime let out a small yelp. He didn't cry, but he crinkled his face.

"We're running out of structures for you to fall from."

Dr. Novak opened a drawer with orthopedic items inside. He grabbed a splint. "I should have a drawer with your name on it."

"Here's clean scissors," Grace said.

As he cut the foam splint to fit the child, Grace helped Jaime into another pair of scrubs to replace his torn and bloodied clothes. She rolled the pants legs up for him. "Sorry, we only have one size." She lifted the sling. "I can do this."

Novak stepped aside as she proceeded to fasten the splint. Then he searched through the medicine cabinet, found two big plastic bottles of pills, and counted out several tablets from each into two small envelopes. "I'm going to give your mom pain medication and antibiotics for you to take." He scribbled instructions in Spanish on the envelopes.

"I know. Come back when I finish them," Jaime said.

"Or if they don't work. Besides, I'll see you as soon as I get an appointment for a cast at Mexicali's clinic."

Novak returned to the medicine cabinet. "One more thing," he said. He readied a tetanus shot and vaccinated Jaime. Then he helped the boy off the exam table, ruffled his hair, and started to escort him and the envelopes out to his parents.

Jaime turned and faced Grace. *"Muchas gracias, señorita."*

Grace smiled at him. "You're welcome."

The two left, and Grace got busy cleaning the room. She threw disposables away, tossed linens into a heap for laundering, put the surgical tools in the sink to wash. She located disinfectant and set about washing down the exam table and the steel trays.

Dr. Novak returned. "You're a nurse, not a janitor," he said.

"Is there anyone else to do it?"

"Me," he said.

"A doctor? That'd be a first." Hearing her words, she bit her lip. Maybe he didn't have a sense of humor.

"I've been doing it for the past five months." He took the sponge from her and ceremoniously began the task.

Amused, Grace watched—until she noticed his biceps flex and his wide shoulders pivot as he put his firm chest and strong legs into the task. What was wrong with her? She'd buried her husband not that long ago.

Mortified, she ran to the sink and poured disinfectant onto the stainless steel tools the doctor had held in his capable hands. What kind of a widow gawked at another man?

"You must be exhausted," he said. "You've had a long flight, probably no meal since breakfast, and you didn't complain once while standing for two hours."

Grace hadn't noticed the ache in her back during the procedure, but she felt it now. She turned to find Dr. Novak leaning against the table, arms crossed over his chest, and his gaze on her. She couldn't read the expression in his green eyes, and she didn't want him reading hers. She turned away. "I guess I am hungry."

He led her out to the narrow hallway.

"I'll show you to your room and let you unpack. Whenever you're ready, I'll take you to the cantina for some food."

A meal sounded heavenly. But Grace wanted to ensure she made a professional first impression. "We can finish in here first."

"We're finished for now. Where are your suitcases?"

"In the waiting room."

She followed him to get her bags and head out to her new home. She felt oddly exhilarated, sensing that she would enjoy her stay in San Felipe.

Novak lifted the luggage easily and turned back toward the exam rooms.

"Where are you going?"

"To put your things in your room."

Grace's gaze followed him down the hallway to two doors at the end.

"Your bedroom is on the left. I sleep to the right," he said.

Her jaw dropped as she stared in disbelief. "My living quarters are *here?*"

He gave her an odd look. "I hope you don't plan to 'live' in your room. I prefer to call them 'sleeping quarters,' meaning, we 'live' out here."

Grace didn't quite understand what he was blathering about. What she did take in was the flimsy wall between their bedrooms. She could probably punch a fist through it. She would certainly be able to hear every move he made. In his bed. And she did not want to think about this man in bed. She bit her lip.

"Is something wrong?" he asked, a hint of annoyance in his voice.

"No. Of course not. I just didn't expect . . . I thought . . ." She licked her lips. "It's fine."

She stepped inside her room. *Get over it. A widow in mourning needn't worry about sleeping arrangements.*

"It's lovely. Thank you."

He set her bags at the threshold. "I hope you didn't expect a four-star hotel," he said grimly. Then he retreated and closed the door.

Feeling stupid, Grace sank onto the bed. It creaked, and she felt her cheeks redden. She was shocked, all right, but not for the reason he presumed.

Actually, though, this glimpse of the doctor's sour attitude might prove a good thing. It would help offset his appealing looks. Grace took a deep breath and glanced around her new abode. The room had a twin bed with a nightstand, one window, one closet, and a dresser. A beautiful comforter covered the bed, and embroidered cloths covered the tops of the dresser and nightstand. The room felt cozy and cared for.

She relaxed a little. Perhaps she'd overreacted, but she hadn't expected to be living so close to her employer during her off hours.

After unpacking, she stood and looked into the tiny wrought-iron–framed mirror. She groaned. Her hair was a mess, and she looked frightful, her makeup completely faded. She changed out of the scrubs and into wrinkled but fresh clothes. She grabbed her handbag and searched for lipstick.

As she raised the lipstick to apply it, she had second thoughts. Instead she took out her brush and dragged it through her hair. As she did so, she thought of her late husband. What would he have thought of her accepting a job in Mexico? Would he be happy for her, or would he call her a coward for fleeing California?

As she spun to exit her room, she spotted a hand-painted ceramic angel above the door. Someone had added that to make Grace feel at home. No doubt the same thoughtful person who had had Father Sanchez pick her up from the airport.

A stab of guilt hit her that she'd concealed her primary reason for coming to Mexico, and Grace had to remember that everything else she'd presented about herself was true. She was a hardworking nurse who would dedicate herself to helping the patients of the clinic.

She felt a little better as she joined Dr. Novak in the waiting room.

"I'll introduce you to some of the villagers. Everyone's eager to meet you," he said, though *he* seemed distinctly unimpressed by her.

"Why's that?" she asked, as he placed his hand on her arm to guide her down the porch steps. She pulled her arm away. He didn't seem to notice.

"You're a part of the clinic, and the clinic's important to the village."

"Why'd you pick me?" Grace couldn't believe she'd asked the question.

"The agency picked you."

"Oh, yes. I forgot," she mumbled. Why did she care who had picked her, as long as she was here?

They left the dirt path for a stone one that led up to a cantina with laughter and lively music spilling from its open windows.

Dr. Novak burst through the swinging doors like a seasoned cowboy entering a saloon. And just like in an old Western, everyone inside instantly quieted and stared at them.

"Here's my nurse, Grace Sinclair."

Everyone jumped up at once and advanced to greet her.

"Bienvenido," a dark-haired woman in her mid-forties greeted Grace. "Welcome to our cantina. I'm Carmen, and this is my husband, Gabriel." Behind the couple a pack of curious villagers swarmed to meet Grace.

Dr. Novak stepped in. "Give Mrs. Sinclair room. She hasn't eaten anything all day." He led her to a table.

"I'll fix her a plate right away," Carmen said.

"What would you like?" Dr. Novak asked Grace.

"Anything."

"Chicken enchiladas?" Carmen asked.

"Yes. Thank you." Grace felt her stomach rumble.

"Same for me," said Novak.

Gabriel carried a tray to their table. From it he set down a pitcher of water, a basket of chips, and a bowl of salsa. He poured a glass of ice water for each of them.

Dr. Novak took a long swallow from his glass. "Would you prefer iced tea?"

"May I get you something else to drink?" Gabriel offered on cue.

"I'm fine with water."

Gabriel hurried away to serve another customer waiting at the bar.

"Everyone's so nice here," Grace said.

Novak dunked a chip into the salsa and popped it into his mouth. He leisurely chewed before speaking. "This village has great food, great people, and a virtually private beach with warm aqua water."

"Sounds like paradise." She sampled the chips and salsa. "Mmm . . . delicious."

"It's paradise for some, but many others live in dire poverty."

"When did you take over the clinic?"

"I didn't take it over. I created it."

Carmen returned with some fresh tortillas and a steaming fajita plate of fixings. "Before heaven sent us this fine doctor, we had no medical care in town. We had to drive our sick all the way to Mexicali." She squeezed Dr. Novak's shoulder and smiled warmly at Grace.

Gabriel passed behind his wife and swatted her butt. Carmen blew a kiss at him. *"Mi amor."*

Grace noted the affection between the two and returned Carmen's smile. All she could think of was the mouthwatering food in front of her. She made a burrito of the fixings, and Dr. Novak watched her eat as he took another swallow of his water.

"That must have been quite a task, opening a clinic in a foreign country," Grace offered. "I'm assuming you're from the States."

He nodded. "There were roadblocks, yes, but if an outcome is important to me, I don't back down from a challenge."

She observed him. Naturally he would be the type who didn't give up until he got what he wanted. She knew that type well—the type she'd vowed to avoid forever. Wasn't that why she'd run away to Mexico? Still, Ryan Novak didn't speak his words with the usual arrogance and bravado of most of the doctors she'd known. He spoke with simple conviction.

"What brought you here in the first place?" Grace imagined he'd visited as a tourist with a pretty girlfriend on his arm.

"A Doctors Without Borders stint. Our team came to give immunizations. I saw the desperate need, especially in the kids."

"I'm impressed," she said, truly meaning it. She bit into her burrito.

"There's a lot more to be done. That's where you come in." He straightened. "I hope you know what you're getting yourself into."

"Meaning what?"

"I'll expect a full day's work from you."

"Why else would I be here . . . to work on my tan?"

"If that's your intention, you may as well pack now."

"I'm not packing, Doctor. You hired me, and I'm here to stay."

They stared at each other, and she sensed his unspoken *We'll see.*

Carmen returned with two plates of savory enchiladas and beans and rice. "Dr. Novak," she tsked, "talk about work later. Let Nurse Sinclair enjoy the dinner."

"You're right," Novak said. "Once you taste Carmen's cooking, you won't ever want to leave."

Grace caught the change in his tone. Did he really expect her to turn tail and run? Of course, if he assumed she wanted a four-star hotel, then she probably would be the type who ran from real work. It was sort of funny that, in her case, she was running *to* work. She dug in.

An hour later Grace dressed for bed. What a day she'd had. As if the long flight from northern California in the tiny eight-seater aircraft with noisy engines wasn't enough, Father Sanchez had greeted her at the airport. Being the novice at deception that she was, she had almost confessed her secret to him.

He'd told Grace that the village of San Felipe needed

Dr. Novak and that Dr. Novak needed her. She would be his only staff.

It seemed she'd come to the right place. No hospital gossips here.

Grace exhaled. Things would be okay. From what she knew about him, Dr. Novak only cared about his patients and the clinic. Just forget that she'd expected an older doctor who had retired to Mexico. Nothing like that mattered, providing she worked hard. And that's what she'd come to do. She'd come to work her tail off learning new skills, escape the painful memories of losing her husband, and get a fresh start.

So far, so good. Only 364 days to go.

A soft rap on the door caused her to jump. That could only be one person. "Yes?" she said, grabbing the comforter to cover herself. It wouldn't do to have her new employer see her dressed in a teddy.

"Do you need anything before I get into bed?"

"I'm fine, thank you." To Grace's dismay, her heart skipped at the tantalizing sound of Ryan Novak's voice.

What's that about? she wondered.

He'd startled her, that's all.

"Good night," he said.

Grace heard him enter his room before she could reply.

He'd startled her, and she was tired. She need only think of her late husband to dispel romantic thoughts about any other man, least of all a doctor. Thinking about her husband now brought a familiar ache to her heart. If only . . .

Chapter Two

The sound of a rooster crowing woke Grace the next morning. The dream of her husband dissipated from her mind. "Wait!" she murmured sleepily. She wanted to hang on to the image. He'd kissed her and held her in his arms, assuring Grace that he loved only her.

The rooster crowed again. Grace sat up, angry with herself. *Don't think about him. And don't you dare miss him.*

Hearing running water, she guessed that Dr. Novak had beaten her to the shower. She opened the window for fresh air and glimpsed a breathtaking view of the Sea of Cortez from her room. "Oh, my!" she murmured. The white sandy beach beckoned her. Grace loved walking on the beach. Or jogging or even just sitting. Swimming was her favorite. But she wondered how much time off she'd have to enjoy the sea.

Well, if she worked hard and exercised hard, she wouldn't have time to feel sorry for herself.

The shower had stopped. Grace selected clothes for the day and opened the hallway door. She hadn't packed a robe. But then, she hadn't anticipated needing one in warm, sunny Mexico. The bathroom door opened, and Grace couldn't turn away from the sight of Ryan Novak wearing only a towel wrapped loosely around his waist. The view from her window paled in comparison. *Darn him.* She scowled.

"Pardon me. I forgot I have a roommate now," he said.

His heated gaze made her skin tingle and abruptly reminded her of the skimpy nightclothes she was wearing.

"Me too." Her cheeks flamed. She wanted to step back into her room and lock herself in. Better to pretend he had no effect on her. She yawned.

He quickly strode to his bedroom and shut the door.

She bolted for the bathroom and took a cool shower.

When she emerged twenty minutes later, she felt much more composed. She wouldn't flatter Ryan Novak by being embarrassed at their encounter. She'd set the tone now for a purely professional relationship.

She heard him in the second exam room. *Time for work.*

"Good morning," she said, as if the hallway incident had never occurred. "Do I smell coffee?"

"Buenos días. It's brewing in my office. Want some?" He wore fluorescent yellow shorts and a colorful Hawaiian-print shirt.

Are we going to a luau? she wondered.

She suddenly felt overdressed in her crisp white uniform. "Sure." She glanced around the second exam room. "This one is set up differently."

"They both have oxygen. This one has tongue depressors, the otoscope, et cetera. The other one is for suturing and setting fractures," he said.

"This one is for medical patients, the other for trauma."

"Yes. I want you to learn exactly where everything is in both rooms in case we need something quickly."

"Like in an emergency room. I understand."

"Though I'll admit, you managed well yesterday," he said. "Let's get that coffee."

She followed him to one of the two remaining doors in the clinic. At the threshold, she decided his "office" had once been a supply closet. "Cozy," she said.

"Not exactly the swank office suite of a California doctor, is it?" He poured coffee into two mugs, and the rich aroma filled the tiny office.

"I wouldn't know. I've never seen one." Her gaze took in the desk with one chair on either side and a four-drawer filing cabinet with the coffeemaker on top. Her apartment building back home had an elevator that was larger than this room.

His artwork intrigued her. Posters of white-water rafters, skiers, and rock climbers took up two walls, while a map of Baja California and personal photographs took up the other. The fourth wall had room only for the door to the hallway.

"What's behind the last door across the hall?"

"A small closet. I keep supplies and the traveling medical bags in there. I'll show you later."

She leaned to get a closer look at his photos when he handed her a mug.

"I have a full day planned for us. We'll take my vehicle to Puertecitos, a village about fifty miles south, to perform physical exams on the children there. We're expected at the church in two hours."

She had so many questions. How did he arrange these

trips? How had he acquired all his equipment? Didn't he have cream or sugar for the coffee?

"Since we may not get lunch, we'd better eat breakfast."

"What happens if we're needed while we're away?"

"Once you're trained, I can leave you behind. Until then, whoever needs me uses the cantina telephone to call my cell phone . . . if it works. Sometimes I'm in too remote a location. But they know where I am and can call that place."

"Like the church."

"Sure, if the church had a phone. You learn to be resourceful out here."

"Will we drive Jaime to Mexicali for a cast?"

"Not today. It usually takes them a couple of days to fit in one of my patients."

Grace wondered how Jaime's family would pay for it. "Well, I'm ready to go."

"Are you sure you want to wear white?"

"I didn't bring black, if that's what you're asking."

"No." Her hasty reply had apparently caught him off guard. He scratched his ear. "You need to be comfortable. It's a bumpy ride, and the village is smaller than this one. It's dustier too."

"I'll be fine—I'm wearing pants, Doctor." Annoyed with herself for feeling vulnerable nonetheless, she brushed past him and out of his office.

After breakfast they loaded supplies into his Jeep Wrangler. Grace marveled at the scenery as they drove, and Ryan enjoyed her enthusiasm. He hadn't seen a trace of the prima donna he'd momentarily glimpsed last night.

But give her time. All women eventually show their true colors. If she weren't an off-limits widow, he wouldn't tolerate having her around for a year.

He felt her gaze on him, and he wondered if she knew about the online contest he'd won.

"You're an adventurer through and through. Were you always like this?" she asked.

"I was a bit like Jaime as a child, I suppose. Falling out of trees, off skateboards and roofs."

"And as an adult?"

"Wind surfing, rock climbing, and snowboarding."

She wrinkled her brow. "Who had more broken bones, you or Jaime?"

"Me. But yesterday he passed me on the stitches."

"Boys will be boys?"

"Girls get into plenty of mischief too. How about you?"

"This job is the most adventurous thing I've ever done."

"Really?" He thought about her recent tragedy. "So what compelled you to make this enormous leap?"

Grace fidgeted in her seat. "I needed a change."

She paused, making him sense the loss she'd suffered and respect the strength she possessed. He stole a glance at her. She wrung her hands. Perhaps he'd been too quick to judge her yesterday.

"And I wanted to improve my skills," Grace added.

"Nursing or kayaking skills?"

She laughed. "Nursing, but the kayaking would be a bonus. I've never tried anything that athletic before."

"You seem athletic."

"I exercise. Swimming and jogging mostly."

He pictured Grace running on the beach and smiled.

"Being fit is a requirement for this job," he said. *So*

is having willpower, he thought, as the image of Grace in her teddy teased his mind. He clutched the steering wheel. Such thoughts were exactly what he had wanted to avoid.

He had been quite clear with the agency. He'd told them, "Send me a mature, level-headed nurse." Ryan hadn't expected a woman quite so young and definitely not so beautiful. He had explained his plight to the agency staff, had told them of his attempts to hire a nurse himself. He had explained the unforeseen complications that winning that contest had caused. The agency staff had reacted with the same amusement as the villagers.

And they'd sent him Grace Sinclair. He watched her as she looked out, marveling at the sea.

"Outdoor exercise will be a reward here," she said.

They passed a blighted village of rough-hewn shacks and rusted, broken-down vehicles. Unwanted items like worn sofas and appliances littered the sides of the road. Grace grew quiet as she observed men and women in worn clothing sitting on old wooden crates outside their meager shacks. Children played tag. The men, wearing sombreros, held their heads high as they watched the Wrangler pass by.

"Why don't we stop here?" she asked. "Those people look as if they could use our help."

"Puertecitos is ten miles farther. We can serve more children from there."

"They have a million-dollar view and probably don't have ten dollars in their pocket," she said. "What do they do for work?"

"The Sea of Cortez villages rely on fishing, some ranching or farming, and tourism."

"Noble professions."

So far Grace Sinclair wasn't anything like the women he'd had to deal with recently. She'd demonstrated that she thought about people other than herself. Her days were occupied with tasks more important than manicures and shopping. Then again, she was a real nurse.

"Will I be traveling alone?"

"No. You'll go with me if I have a large number of people to see. Otherwise you'll hold down the fort in San Felipe."

"What's the plan when we arrive at the church? We don't have much in the way of medical equipment with us."

"We're not performing the type of physical you're familiar with. Mine doesn't include lab tests or X-rays." He pointed behind him. "Grab that clipboard, and look at the checklist I developed."

Grace retrieved the clipboard and perused the checklist. "You're assessing the child's health in general. Eyes, ears, tonsils. Vital signs. Height and weight."

"We're introducing ourselves so that the townspeople know we're here. I can also examine any child who is ill. And I'm getting an idea of the medical resources they need."

"You mean like dental work or immunizations?"

"The grant funders who support La Clínica Pediátrica want to know the number of children we're serving. But we need to know who all our potential patients are. Do we need ten size small nasal cannulas or twenty? And you're right. We can inform other agencies of how many vaccines we need or let the Dentists Without Borders know what the demand is."

"I see immunizations listed here," she said.

"We won't be administering any today."

"What if we encounter seriously ill patients?"

"Of course I'll make referrals if a patient requires something out of the clinic's scope."

"How large of an area do you expect us to serve?"

"Most villagers don't have reliable vehicles. I figure an hour drive, at the most, is what they can reasonably travel."

"Or us, in an emergency?"

"Or us." Ryan hadn't used the terms *us* or *we* so often as he had since Grace had arrived. It felt strange. Not that he was a *me* kind of guy. But he'd always thought of the clinic as *his*. Now he had to get used to sharing it.

"My long-term goal is to serve one hundred miles in each direction; that'll cover thirty villages that are too far from a major city. Right now I see us handling fifty miles each way. I'll show you the map in my office, but basically it's as far as Puertecitos to the south, Santa Clara to the west, and La Trinidad to the north."

"Once more, I'm impressed. You've got everything figured out," she said. He noticed a hint of admiration in her voice.

If she only knew, he thought, *that I've been figuring things out as I go.*

"Here we are." He slowed the Wrangler to a stop. With no paved roads or sidewalks in town, a dust cloud had formed around them. Grace waved the dust away.

Puertecitos' population of eighty-six seemed to consist mostly of young children. The small, weathered village fell somewhere between the more developed San Felipe and the ramshackle village they'd passed ten miles back.

Several children played with a soccer ball in front of the church, dirt puffing up all around them.

A boy kicked the ball away from a girl, and the ball flew at Grace. In a fluid motion she brought up her right leg, stopped the ball with her instep, and kicked it back. The kids squealed with delight.

"Okay, now I'm impressed. Are there any other secrets you left off your application?" Ryan teased.

Grace's shocked expression alarmed him.

Crap. Now what? he thought.

A barefoot girl in tattered clothing with hair falling loose from her ponytail ran up to Grace and spoke excitedly in Spanish.

Grace bent to the girl's height and discovered that the child wanted to know how to do that fancy move.

"After we're done with work?" she asked Ryan. But the little girl was already pulling Grace into the soccer game. "I'll be quick," she called over her shoulder to him.

Normally he'd shake off his suspicion. But his instincts had sharpened lately, and he recognized that guilty look on Grace's face. What secret could she be keeping?

He watched her playing with the kids. She behaved like a saint. Had the face of an angel.

Hadn't he learned by now that those innocent traits could be the worst? He intended to find out what the heck Grace Sinclair had to hide. He wasn't about to let anyone jeopardize his clinic.

He'd question her until she came clean. He removed a case of supplies from the back of the Wrangler. He'd watch her every move and uncover her true motive for coming here.

"Grace!" he called. A kid kicked the ball right at him. With his hands full, he could only duck. Still, the ball smacked him square on the forehead and bounced back to the kids. They laughed.

"Are you okay?" Grace tried concealing her smile as she continued playing.

"I'm fine." Maybe he shouldn't suspect a saint of sinning in front of a church. Next time it could be a bolt of lightning striking him.

He heard a chorus of moans as Grace left the kids and approached him. Her eyes sparkled at him.

Clear your head, Novak. Stop jumping to conclusions. After all, the agency had done a thorough background check.

"You have a big red circle on your forehead," she said as she plucked the other case from the Jeep.

"That should make a great first impression on the villagers."

She giggled. A sexy little laugh that made his gut twitch. Father Morales came outside and greeted them. "We have a community room in the back of the church." He took Grace's case. "There is also a small private room if you need it."

"Thank you, Father."

In the back courtyard, a line of villagers young and old had begun to form.

"There's adults here too," Grace said.

"That's permissible. We'll see everyone."

Four hours later, less than a handful of people waited. Ryan and Grace had seen patients from three villages. Father Morales had done a great job of getting the word out.

Ryan glanced at Grace. She had taken the vital signs of all their patients the old-fashioned way, with a stethoscope and sphygmomanometer. Presently her fingers were on a pregnant woman's wrist as she took her radial pulse and respirations.

Grace jotted down the results on the checklist and rose. She spoke softly to the woman before approaching Ryan.

"I had considered myself fluent in Spanish, but I think I just increased my vocabulary by at least twenty words." Grace placed the checklist in front of him. "Her blood pressure's high, and her face is flushed."

"I heard you do a lot of chatting with the kids."

"They're great." Grace ushered the woman's husband into the room.

"Mucho gusto." Ryan shook the couple's hands. He asked how many children they had, noting that the woman was diaphoretic.

"Cinco," the woman said.

"Five," Grace repeated, taking notes for him as he conducted the exam.

"Did you have high blood pressure with your earlier pregnancies?"

"Yes, the last one," the husband answered in Spanish. "But never the cramps that she has now."

Ryan shot a glance at Grace as he asked the woman, "Are you taking medication for the blood pressure or anything else?"

"No."

"Describe the pain. Is it constant, or does it come and go? Is it sharp or dull?"

The woman answered.

"Are you bleeding?"

"No."

"Have the baby's movements changed since the pain started?"

The woman motioned with her hands as she explained.

He breathed a sigh of relief. Grace watched him observantly. He turned to face her.

"I got it," Grace said. "The cramps started today and are irregular and dull. She's not on medications. There's no bleeding, and the baby's still active." Grace scribbled notes on the back of the checklist.

Ryan asked more questions as he took the fetal heart rate. "Sounds good."

The woman replied that a midwife had delivered all her babies. She only saw a doctor for the last delivery because she got sick.

Ryan turned to the couple. "I need to examine the cervix."

Grace closed the door of the small room and opened the cot. The husband helped his wife get situated.

It only took Ryan a moment to determine that effacement had not occurred and the cervix had not dilated.

"Is everything okay?" the husband asked.

"Yes. She can get up." Ryan removed his gloves. "Your wife has pregnancy-induced hypertension. I'm prescribing medication for the high blood pressure. Do you remember what she took last time, or if it caused any side effects?"

The husband handed him an empty pill bottle. *"No problemas."*

Ryan took the bottle as if it were the Holy Grail, praising the husband for keeping it. He read the label: *Cata-*

pres. "She needs complete bed rest until her delivery in one month." Ryan had to explain what *bed rest* meant.

Thank heaven he'd brought some of every medication he stocked with them. "Write *thirty-day supply of Catapres* on her chart, please." He counted out the tablets into an envelope.

The kids who had been playing soccer were their final, reluctant patients. Their parents had rounded them up and brought them in for physicals.

"Check his ears," one mother said. "He never hears me when I call him."

"Is that so? Then I have a test for him." He dug out a large syringe from the case. "Here we go."

"No!" the boy gasped. "I pretend I can't hear her, but I can!"

His mother understood enough to give her rowdy youngster a soft whack on the arm.

"Ouch!"

Ryan turned away before the boy saw his smile.

Father Morales offered them a cup of tea before they hit the road. They accepted. The tea soothed Ryan almost as much as Grace's calm nature had throughout the exams, he mused.

As they loaded the cases into the Wrangler, the church bells clanged.

"Oh, I forgot," Ryan said. "Father Morales asked if we wanted any services . . . like confession . . . before we left."

Grace blinked at him. "No, but thank you."

"That's what I thought."

He watched Grace divert her gaze before she slid into the Jeep.

Ryan decided against questioning her. He had no doubt that she was an adequate nurse, and he needed her for his clinic. If Grace turned out to be a gold digger after his contest winnings, the laugh would be on her when she discovered he had no money left. In fact, he'd never been more broke in his life.

Chapter Three

Grace needed this job. She couldn't risk her employer's finding any reason to send her back to California. *I positively cannot return until I'm ready—after I've recovered.*

Maybe she would never recover. That thought frightened her, and she shoved it aside.

Grace pulled open the top drawer in the medical exam room. An assortment of antibacterial creams and ointments rested beside samples of dermatological cleansers and analgesic lotions. Small medicated bandages, gauze, and cotton balls took up space next to inactivated ice packs. "Skin treatment," Grace noted aloud, opening the next drawer.

Larger bandages, gauze pads, and dressing tape shared room with alcohol pads, iodine swabs, and cotton-tipped applicators. She could add *organized* and *meticulous* to Dr. Novak's list of attributes.

The third drawer down held a wide variety of syringes and needles. As she scanned the contents to determine the doctor's filing system, he strode in.

"Figure out where everything is yet?"

She glanced up. He wore bright orange shorts and a Picasso-like cotton shirt. She lifted her gaze from his leather sandals.

"Your storage arrangement is different in here compared to your surgical exam room."

"What's my methodology?"

"The types of ailments you expect to treat?"

"Simpler. The most commonly used items at the top," he said. "Have you perused the cabinets over the sink?"

"Not in this room."

"That can wait. Are you ready for an in-depth orientation to La Clínica Pediátrica's operations?"

"Absolutely." Her stomach fluttered in anticipation.

Grace took notes as he explained his clinic practices. "Most folks don't make appointments. They just pop in. For patients needing a follow-up, I like to get those done first thing in the morning. Twice a week, I . . . we'll travel."

Three hours later she asked, "How have you managed alone for so long?" He did everything from making house calls to ordering supplies to paying the bills to mopping the floors. She'd never met a doctor that dedicated. Her husband had certainly never mopped floors or ordered supplies.

"That's the problem. I've just been 'managing'—barely. I want to do more outreach, more instruction, and acquire more resources."

"I'm not afraid of hard work, Doctor. Feel free to pass on *any* of your duties to me." She'd readily do windows for this man. Anything to free up his time for the important tasks he performed.

"I appreciate that," he said. "I guess you're not a prima donna."

Grace chuckled. "Hardly."

He reviewed all her duties and his expectations of her. None included household chores. She'd help out anyway. He had very high standards and expected a great deal of himself.

Next he quizzed her on the location of several items. She missed two out of ten. He gave her homework.

He reiterated that they were on call twenty-four hours a day, seven days a week. If they were needed, they would respond.

"Here's your training calendar." He presented Grace with a list of pediatric techniques splayed over a calendar.

"This is an ambitious schedule. I'm pleased," she said. "I always wanted to specialize in pediatrics, but the openings were few. I guess pediatric nurses stay in their assignments for a long time." She waved the page at him. "This training program is very exciting." It would give her the year's experience she needed to get a coveted slot back home.

"You'll be so well-trained, I won't want to let you go in a year," he said, eying her.

Grace glanced back at the schedule, not wanting him to see her pain. She hoped she hadn't visibly squirmed at his comment, but the exclamation had touched a nerve. Hadn't her husband spoken similar words about never letting her go?

"Good thing we have a contract. So we both know

exactly when my time's up," she said. *It saves the humiliation of being dumped out of the blue. Or worse. Her husband had definitely done far worse.*

"Of course the contract can be severed if you fail to meet the quality standards."

"That won't happen," Grace said. She'd never failed when it came to work.

"I like your confidence."

"And I like your foresight." She scanned the training calendar. He was serious about wanting a qualified nurse. That knowledge allowed her to relax in his company.

"The contract can also be severed if you lied about your credentials or background."

She didn't like the way he'd said that, and she didn't like the way his gaze narrowed on her. "Doctor, are you actually accusing me of lying? That's quite an insult." Her blood pressure rose, and she felt her nostrils flare. "I have never falsified—"

Voices from outside caught their attention. Heavy footsteps bounded up the wooden porch stairs.

Dr. Novak swiftly opened the door. Gabriel, the cantina owner, held a limp child in his arms. Carmen caught up with them, out of breath.

Grace guessed the child was about five years old.

"What happened to Chiquita?" Novak asked, as he checked her pupils while leading them to the medical exam room.

Grace hurried alongside them. The child was pale and appeared to be unconscious.

"She came running into the cantina crying," Carmen said. "She showed me her arm."

"A bee sting?" Dr. Novak asked, examining the swollen site on her arm.

"*Sí,*" Gabriel said.

"She was wheezing, then suddenly she collapsed," Carmen said.

As Gabriel laid Chiquita on the exam table, Dr. Novak slipped his hand under her neck and lifted, opening her airway. He took her radial pulse. "Tachycardic."

Grace observed the blue lips and fingernails. Hives had broken out on Chiquita's pale skin. Worse, it was difficult to tell whether she was breathing at all. Grace slipped a rolled towel under the girl's neck to free Dr. Novak's hand.

Dr. Novak continued his quick assessment. He opened her mouth and inspected her throat for any obstruction. Then he confirmed Chiquita's apnea. "Bag her!"

Grace grabbed the Ambu bag with a small face mask. She tilted the girl's head, placed the mask over her face, and rhythmically squeezed the bag.

"She's not breathing! My baby's not breathing!" Alarm strained Carmen's voice.

Dr. Novak gave Gabriel a firm look.

The man understood and held his wife back. "*El doctor* will help her."

Dr. Novak opened the medicine cabinet and pulled out a vial and a needle. He filled a syringe. "I'm pushing three cc's of epinephrine."

"What's that for?" Carmen shouted.

"Please trust me, Carmen," Dr. Novak said. He administered the medicine. "She has anaphylaxis. She must be allergic to bee stings."

Grace didn't pause in squeezing the Ambu bag.

As they all watched Chiquita, Gabriel kept a gentle but firm grasp on his frazzled wife. "How can a little bee cause this?"

"Anaphylactic shock is a severe reaction to the venom in the sting." He took over squeezing the Ambu bag and told Grace, "She needs Benadryl IV to stop the histamine reaction."

Grace started an IV and administered the medication.

"It was as if someone was choking her—she was suffocating right in front of me," Gabriel said, clutching his wife's hand.

Grace returned to the Ambu bag.

"Her throat swelled closed." Novak took the girl's pulse as he talked. "She's going to be fine. Her vital signs are already returning to normal."

"One hundred percent O-two," he said to Grace.

Grace opened a nasal cannula, connected the tubing to a wall oxygen unit, turned the dial to 100%, and administered it to Chiquita. The sound of air hissing filled the room, and within a few minutes Chiquita's eyes fluttered open.

"*Hola,* Chiquita." Dr. Novak used the stethoscope to check her heart and lungs.

She raised a hand. "Hi."

"*Hija!*" *Daughter!* Carmen and Gabriel became ecstatic.

Dr. Novak glanced at Grace, who now stood with the epinephrine vial and a syringe, ready to dispense a second dose. "That won't be necessary," he said. "Take her vitals every five minutes times three, then every ten times four."

"Yes, Doctor."

He moved out of the way so Chiquita's parents could come nearer. "I want to keep her under observation for two hours. During that time I'll teach you what certain symptoms mean, so you'll know how to respond if this happens again."

Gabriel nodded and hugged his wife.

"I'll get an allergy kit for you to keep at home when I go into Mexicali."

"Muchas gracias, Doctor." Gabriel shook Dr. Novak's hand.

It dawned on Grace that Chiquita would have died without Dr. Novak's aid.

Carmen threw her arms around Novak in a tight, tearful embrace. "You can have free enchiladas forever!"

Dr. Novak laughed. "I'll accept one dinner for me and my nurse."

Everyone turned to smile at Grace—and they all caught her gazing at Dr. Novak. Her gaze met his, and for a moment the only sound came from the hissing oxygen equipment.

Chiquita moaned, taking the spotlight off Grace.

Her parents hugged her. Dr. Novak spoke reassuringly as he examined her neuro reflexes. Grace knew what her own neurological reflexes would be if Dr. Novak touched her as compassionately!

But that wasn't the way she wanted to be touched by him or any doctor.

As if *she'd* been stung by a deadly bee, Grace recoiled from him.

He didn't notice.

Hearing movement coming from the waiting room, Grace eagerly left to investigate. Several villagers with concerned faces had crept onto the porch and into the clinic, waiting to hear the status of young Chiquita.

"Chiquita *es bien*," Grace said. *She's fine.*

The crowd seemed to collectively breathe a sigh of relief. Then they eyed her curiously. One dark beauty in her early twenties pushed her way forward. She scrutinized Grace before offering her hand.

"I'm Benita."

"Nice to meet you." Grace smiled, happy to find someone near her age. The woman smiled back.

After the crowd had dispersed and Chiquita had gone home with her parents, Dr. Novak approached Grace.

"I could use a walk. How about you?"

"Let me change my shoes."

"You can change your clothes too. I appreciate the professional uniform, but you're making me look bad."

Grace chuckled. "Believe me, nothing can make you look bad in the eyes of these villagers."

"Is that so?"

"I've only met a handful of them, but they obviously all adore you."

"That's because I'm the only doctor. I bet the only mechanic and the only plumber get the same adoration."

"Your humility is refreshing."

"A nurse must see humility every day."

"Not from doctors." She disappeared down the hallway to her room.

"I suppose my species does have a bad reputation," he called.

"Ha!" Grace closed the door. He had no idea!

Discarding her uniform, she slipped into shorts, a T-shirt, and jogging shoes. She brushed and refastened her hair in the ponytail.

"Much better," he said when she rejoined him. "Before we go, let me apologize if I sounded like I accused you of lying."

"Thank you. I assure you my credentials and work experience are genuine."

"Okay. Good."

Grace wondered what had made him suspicious in the first place, but she let the incident go.

Outside, the warm sun gleamed down on San Felipe and its inhabitants. Children ran and played. Adults stayed busy. Two men on a rooftop hammered away. Women fed chickens and pigs. A man placed crates of fresh produce out on a rickety display cart. Three teenagers had their heads under a car hood.

A woman sweeping her porch waved at them.

"That's the general store," he said. They waved back.

A nice office building ahead had a few people coming and going.

"That's the bank. I'll introduce you to Poncho and later his wife, Petra. They own my clinic building and most of the town."

Dr. Novak opened the door for her. The quaint-looking bank had tile floors, wrought-iron chandeliers, and lots of woodwork.

A large man in his sixties rose from a desk behind a glass wall to welcome them. *"Doctor, bienvenidos."* They exchanged a firm handshake. "This must be Nurse Sinclair. It is good to finally meet you."

"Please call me Grace," she said, taking his proffered hand.

He wore an expensive embroidered shirt and brown slacks with a wide leather belt and leather boots. His intelligent eyes had a glimmer in them.

"Please come to the ranch and meet my wife and family."

"That sounds nice, thank you."

"When is the next poker game? I want to win my money back from you," Poncho said to Dr. Novak.

"I'm glad you asked. I need some cash for allergy kits."

Poncho shook his head. "*El doctor* looks like a kind man. But in a poker game, he is ruthless."

Dr. Novak jabbed Poncho's shoulder. "Thursday night."

"*Excelente*. Hold on to your wallet."

They said good-bye.

Once outside, Grace spoke. "Don't tell me poker is funding your clinic operations."

"Lady, you have no idea how I manage to stay afloat."

Grace studied him for a moment.

"You're thinking I'm a phony. Respectable doctor on the outside, hustler on the inside."

"No." Though that description had fit her husband, she couldn't yet decide if it fit Dr. Novak. "I'm thinking your grant funding isn't adequate and we need to apply for more."

"I hoped you could help in that area."

"I saw it on my checklist. Perhaps we should move it up in priority. I've never done grant writing before, but I can learn."

"I appreciate your optimistic attitude."

"It's the only way to get anything done," she said.

"I agree completely. Let's finish exploring the town square."

He showed her where to get things, who did what, and who lived where. He revealed more of himself in his descriptions than he realized. And the more Grace learned about Ryan Novak, the more intrigued she became. He certainly had the respect of the townspeople. He knew everyone's names, even the kids. They flocked around him and excitedly asked him questions.

"Why aren't they in school?"

"There's a one-room schoolhouse connected to the church. All the kids share it, and the different classes take turns." He glanced at his watch. "Right now middle school is in session."

"Can't rooms be added to the existing structure?"

"One cause at a time." He smiled at her. They walked toward the church plaza and faced a small Spanish-style structure beside the pristine adobe church. He pointed at the beige school building. "La Escuela de San Felipe."

The cared-for schoolhouse looked sturdy and prominent, but she noted the absence of any playground apparatus or basketball courts.

"The villagers must take great pride in having a school. And there's room for expansion," she said.

"Room to grow. That's a good motto for San Felipe."

Later, in the cantina, Grace finished her filling meal. "Do you eat here every day?"

"I like being in the true hub of the town. Everything happens here in the cantina, it houses the village telephone, and the food's the best."

She had to agree on the last. No dish she'd tried yet

had disappointed her. The patrons were friendly. Some-one always had an interesting story to tell.

"Why don't they ever bring you a bill?" she asked.

"They put it on my tab. I pay every couple of weeks." He took a drink of his water.

"I can buy my own meals."

Dr. Novak brought his glass down on the table. "Absolutely not. Your agreement includes room and board, and I insist on providing it."

"Well, if you feel that strongly about it."

"I do. I honor my word."

"I see that." She'd figured that part out herself. She knew instinctively he was a *doctor* who could be counted on, but what about the *man?* Not that it concerned her.

"Do women get in on the poker action?" she asked.

"No."

"Why not?"

He shrugged. "It's tradition."

Grace had no interest in poker, but she liked the way her question seemed to bother the good doctor.

"Anyone with money should be allowed to join the game."

He shook his head. "A woman would be bad luck. I'll give you extra homework if you need something to do."

His comment now ruffled *her* feathers. "I have other things on my plate. My life doesn't revolve around you." *Oops.* She shouldn't have said that.

He arched his eyebrows. "I think it does, actually."

She wanted to break his water glass over his head. Anything to get that smirk off his face. "Maybe. Some of the time."

"Twenty-four/seven."

"How long have you been in Mexico? Because you seem to have the macho thing down pat."

He laughed. "Grace . . ."

"Don't worry. I'm not interested in poker." Nor was she interested in spending more time with a cocky, demanding doctor than necessary.

"Are you sure?" he asked.

Grace glanced at him, mortified. She hadn't spoken aloud, had she? "Sure?" she echoed.

"No more arguments about poker?"

"Of course not. It's not like we're married." She needed training on not always voicing her thoughts.

He chuckled.

Carmen passed their table carrying a tray of margaritas for some tourists sitting in the courtyard. The frosty drinks looked appetizing. If she were in a festive mood, she'd order one. Right now she felt disconcerted. The last time she'd had a cocktail was with her husband. She pushed aside the angst rising within.

"I got a call from Mexicali. We can drive Jaime up tomorrow," Dr. Novak said, bringing her attention back to him.

"That's great." Maybe she *should* order a cocktail. To prove she could have one without feeling miserable over her husband.

She wished it were that easy to get him out of her system.

Carmen returned. She pointed discreetly at the table of tourists. Boisterous laughter came from the courtyard. "Warning: *turista* alert!"

Her words perplexed Grace. "Huh?"

"This one's *loca*." *A nut.* Carmen seemed excited, like

a person ready to watch a football game on TV. Pure anticipation.

Dr. Novak sat up straight. "Grace, I might need a favor. Can you pretend to be my girlfriend?"

Chapter Four

Grace blinked at him. Ryan knew he had no right to ask her to lie for him.

A tipsy blond bumped into their table. *"Hola.* Aren't you that hottie Dr. Novak?"

"Excuse me, but you're interrupting a date," he said.

The blond glanced at Grace. "How much fun can a girl who drinks iced tea be?"

"You'd be surprised," Grace said.

Ryan's eyebrows shot up.

The woman planted her hands on her hips. "My name is Mandy. May I join you?"

Carmen set another tea-filled glass in front of Grace. Grace lifted the drink to her lips and swallowed. The way she savored the liquid had Ryan wondering why he hadn't noticed her sumptuous mouth before.

"Uh . . . ," Ryan stammered.

Mandy touched his arm. "Is that a yes?"

"Actually . . . no." *Please make this sloshed woman go away,* he thought.

"You're hotter than your photographs. Will you autograph one for me?"

Grace paused in mid-sip.

Ryan squirmed.

"What photographs?" Grace asked, after another sip.

Mandy looked at her disbelievingly. "You can't fool me. I'd recognize this bod anywhere." She squeezed his biceps.

Grace coughed on her tea.

"The photos are in my room. I'd love it if you'd sign one for me."

Ryan didn't know what shocked him more—the audacity of the woman, or his noticing Grace's kissable mouth.

"Sorry, he's with me," Grace said.

"I paid my five bucks. And I made my friends vote. The least you can do is . . ."

"Paid for what?" Grace asked. She licked her lips.

He didn't want her to find out like this.

"Sure. I'll sign. Let's go to your room." Ryan jumped up. He shouldn't have involved Grace. What was he thinking?

"Hey, you can't leave with this floozy."

"Who're you calling a floozy?"

"If you're inviting another woman's date to your room, count on being called names."

"Grace, it's okay," Ryan said.

"It's not okay. You've already said no," Grace said.

Damn, what had he done?

"If the doctor wants to come to my room, that's his business."

"He arrived with me, so he leaves with me." Grace stood.

"You're not his type," Mandy said.

"Neither are you," Grace replied.

Mandy's friends had gathered. Carmen grabbed an empty frying pan as she stepped to Grace's side. Gabriel appeared beside her. Benita stood nearby.

Things were spiraling out of control.

"Graciela, are you okay?" Carmen asked.

"Apparently she's not. She needs someone *else* to walk her home," Mandy said. She looped her arm in Ryan's.

Ryan immediately eluded her grasp. He wasn't interested in Mandy. He only wanted to get her the heck away from Grace.

A patron walked by and bumped Mandy into jostling the table.

In a surreal scene, Mandy pushed Grace, and Grace started to retaliate. Ryan moved fast. He grabbed Grace from behind and pulled her away just as she swung. Her fist narrowly missed Mandy's jaw.

His admiration for Grace increased tenfold. Ryan tossed her over his shoulder and carried her out. The crowd broke out in applause and hoots and hollers. Carmen cheered with her upraised frying pan.

"Come back!" Mandy shouted. "I'm not through with you!"

Ryan wondered if Mandy was shouting for him or Grace.

"Hey, put me down." Grace wriggled on his shoulder.

Ryan increased his pace. "Not yet."

"Is this how you repay a favor?"

He put her down. "You did do all that for me, didn't you?" he mused aloud.

"Actually," Grace said, "I did it for our patients. We have

a long drive tomorrow." She crossed her arms. "Would you really have gone to that woman's room?"

"It's not what you're thinking."

"You expected her to make a pass at you. What's going on, Doctor? Because frequently having to defend your honor will definitely be a cause for renegotiation of my salary."

He laughed despite himself. He shook his head and guided her to the clinic's porch.

"Have a seat." Ryan sat on the stoop and patted the floor. Grace sat beside him.

"Remember, earlier, I said I'd done some strange things to keep afloat?"

"How could I forget?"

"Did I mention I have an enterprising younger brother? He's a graduate business student at UCLA. Chad's very talented and creative."

Grace watched him skeptically.

He took a deep breath. "Chad invented this crazy scheme to get my clinic more money. I went along with it because the clinic desperately needed equipment and supplies."

"Go on."

"He developed a Web site contest. He called it the 'Sexiest Doctor in the World' contest. Somehow he got about forty doctors to enter, and he and his college buddies promoted it. Voters all across America and a few foreign countries paid five bucks per ballot and a dollar to download photos. Miraculously, over sixteen thousand people cast votes."

"And you won?"

He heard a hint of disappointment in her question.

"Can you believe it?" He still couldn't.

Grace digested the news. "Don't tell me you have a fan club."

Clearly, she was not at all pleased. The idea seemed to disgust her.

"Incredibly, yes." He'd been dumbfounded when the fan mail arrived. "Initially it seemed funny. But now, with a pushy, in-person autograph request, it seems kind of creepy."

"Why did you really reject Mandy?"

Her question puzzled him.

"Don't answer. I don't want to know." She stood abruptly. "Count me out of your game, Doctor."

He stood and blocked her path. "Grace."

She gazed up at him.

"It's not a game. Not to me." He ran a hand through his hair. "The contest has been both a blessing and a disaster."

"Right. Gorgeous women flinging themselves at you is a disaster. Poor Dr. Novak."

"Why are you so upset?"

Grace caught herself. She looked away. "It's your life. If that's how you want to spend your leisure time . . ."

"I don't have 'leisure time.' If I did, I wouldn't want to spend it with immature money grubbers." Ryan had decided that the prize money had to be what his female fans were after. What else could make women write love letters to a stranger? "I've had my share of conniving women."

"Except when they connive for your benefit?"

She had a point. But Ryan got the impression that he'd hurt her somehow. "I know that I shouldn't have asked you to lie for me. I wasn't thinking, and it won't happen again."

"I'm not the one who needs your repentance."

"Meaning?"

"Mandy participated in a charitable cause. You treated her horribly. You have to go back to the cantina and apologize to her."

"What?" He wasn't the one who'd tried to punch her in the nose.

"And while you're at it, sign whatever she wants."

"No way. I don't want to encourage her."

Grace looked incredibly cute when she got worked up. He might not have seen this side of her had he not crossed the line.

"Don't worry—Carmen will be there to protect you," Grace mocked. "Listen. Mandy donated to the clinic. She picked you out of forty men. Show some class, and sign her photo."

Ryan watched her eyes flare. He smiled. "Remind me not to ask you to be my girlfriend again. It makes you rowdy."

Grace took a step forward and stood toe to toe with him. She tilted her chin and looked him directly in the eye. "Stop changing the subject. You were wrong. I was wrong. One of us needs to apologize, and it isn't going to be me."

He arched his eyebrows in surprise. "Since you put it that way . . ." Ryan wished he could lean down and kiss her sweet, pouty mouth. He savored gazing at her up close. With her hair tousled and her eyes sparking, Grace looked more appealing than ever. Her scent beckoned him, and he decided he'd willingly fulfill any request she made.

"I hoped I could count on you to behave honorably," she said.

He snapped out of his stupor.

Honorably? If she only knew his *dis*honorable thoughts. What was with him, thinking about kissing her? That was just the sort of trouble he sought to prevent.

"All right." Ryan almost suggested they flip a coin to see who went back, but she was likely to take a swing at him. "You have a nasty right hook."

"It's nothing compared to my jabs."

"I believe you. You're a dangerous woman, Grace."

Dr. Novak returned to the cantina while Grace went back to her room. She took a shower to cool off, literally. It didn't help. His words had stuck in her mind. Why had it upset her so much when he revealed his contest dilemma? Dr. Novak was a single man, free to entertain as many women as he chose. It had nothing to do with her.

Yet she hadn't liked seeing Mandy entice him to come to her room. It reminded Grace of other unpleasant observations she'd shoved to the back of her mind. Painful discoveries that had hurt nearly as much as losing her husband. Her heart ached. If she'd been more like Mandy, flirtatious and bold, maybe she'd still have her husband by her side.

Slowly she approached her dresser and opened the top drawer. She retrieved a photo of her husband and herself. The two of them smiled happily in the only picture she'd kept. Grace had never loved a man more. She had given him everything. And he had loved her back. At least he *looked* like a man in love in the photo. But now he was gone. Forever. Her chest tightened. "I wish I could talk to you," she whispered. She had so many unanswered questions. The only thing she knew for sure was that she hadn't really known him at all.

Oh, she'd thought she knew him. Or, rather, she'd fooled herself into believing she knew what made him tick. But she knew as much about Dr. Novak as she did about her own husband. And there were far too many similarities.

In fact, Dr. Novak was worse. He'd been arrogant enough to enter a sexy-doctor contest! She doubted he'd participated with the sole objective of raising money for his clinic. How clever to ensure a steady stream of women falling over themselves for him. Well, she wasn't going to be one of them. Grace didn't care how many votes he had garnered. The last thing she needed was a celebrity doctor with a big, fat ego.

Grace glanced at her clock. He'd been gone over an hour. Why had she sent him back to that vile, loose woman? Mandy had obviously convinced the doctor to stay with her awhile. Maybe even for the night. Grace closed her mind to the images popping up. Images of Dr. Novak tearing off his and Mandy's clothes.

Grace remembered what Dr. Novak looked like without a shirt. She understood why women had eagerly paid their dollars for a photo of his bare chest to admire in private as often as they wanted. *Get over it, Grace.* It's just a chest with toned muscles and curly wisps of hair. It's just strong shoulders and arms capable of easily lifting her and carrying her off to his . . .

That did it. She needed a walk. Already dressed in

shorts and T-shirt, Grace tied her jogging sneakers. With purpose, she barged through the clinic and out the door . . . and straight into the chest of the man she least wanted to see.

"Going somewhere?" he said.

Grace caught her breath. "For a walk . . . alone." She walked past him, but he joined her.

"You can't walk alone at night."

"I like solitary walks."

"Then take them during the day."

"I will." She quickened her pace. He effortlessly kept stride with her.

"I'm glad you convinced me to see Mandy. She's a great gal."

"I can only imagine."

"We laughed about the whole thing, and we talked about you."

Grace shot him a glance. He was cool, in control. She wouldn't take the bait. "How nice."

"We hit it off. She isn't mad at us."

"Now I can sleep."

"I signed her pictures. She had three."

It took an hour to sign three photos?

"Then I posed for a few pictures with her."

Grace wouldn't go there.

"Her friends are entertaining too. In fact, you and I have a date with them Sunday night."

"What?"

"It'll be fun."

"I don't want to be dragged to your soirée."

"You need a mental-health break. I insist."

"You do a lot of insisting, don't you, Doctor?"

He shrugged.

"I prefer reviewing my Spanish lessons."

"We'll all talk in Spanish for the evening."

"Do you enjoy annoying me?" Grace hadn't meant to say the words aloud. Dr. Novak seemed to bring out the impulsiveness in her.

"You annoy *me* for the most peculiar reasons. Skip the Spanish lessons. You need to learn some friendliness."

"Ouch. You've got a mean jab too." But Grace had deserved that one. "I just meant that I'd be a party pooper. Without me you can eat, drink, and be merry." She didn't want to witness the hussy Mandy all over Dr. Novak. Or, worse, see him enjoying it.

"You're my protection."

"A big, strong doctor like you can take care of yourself."

"Not from the clutches of a determined woman. Only having you at my side will do."

"Shall I bring garlic?"

"Whatever helps."

Grace laughed. Ryan Novak obviously could handle himself. For whatever reason—probably because he didn't want Mandy to get too attached—he'd asked Grace to join them.

"A mental-health break it is," she said, as they arrived back at the clinic and sat on the porch.

"You've got yourself a date with the sexiest doctor in the world."

She groaned. "Don't you mean the goofiest doctor?"

He laughed, and Grace enjoyed the rich sound. She could see how a woman might get caught up in his charm.

But she wouldn't. The stupidest thing she could do was let herself fall for this doctor.

Didn't she have a mantra? She couldn't recall the words. But that didn't matter. All she needed to remember was that she could not hang on to her own husband for more than two years. Certainly a dynamic man like the one at her side would crush her heart.

"I appreciate your rationality, Grace."

That had to be the least romantic line anyone had ever said. Maybe he wasn't a womanizer.

"You and your brother must have driven your mom crazy." If Chad had half the charm and looks of his big brother, Grace wondered how their mother had kept the girls off them long enough for them to study.

"As a matter of fact, we did. But she always kept one step ahead of us." He leaned back on the porch, making himself comfortable. "My brother always had some scheme up his sleeve. He'll do great in business."

"I'm sure you were the example."

"Why does everyone assume that?" he said in feigned defensiveness.

"Let's just say I have a feeling Chad plays poker in his college dorm."

He laughed. "You sound like my mother."

Grace smiled at the warmth in his voice. *Now* there's *a compliment.* She rose before she latched on to his arm and batted her lashes as Mandy had. "Good night."

"Sleep tight. Don't let *las cucarachas* bite," he said.

She clamped her mouth shut. She did not blurt out that cockroaches were the least of her worries.

Chapter Five

Early the next morning Grace awoke to the sounds of cabinets in the nearest exam room opening and closing. Dr. Novak had already begun work.

She opened her window to the view of the sea. Fishermen set out on their small boats, pursuing their livelihood. Grace longed to visit the beach but still hadn't had the opportunity. It seemed no matter how early she awoke, the good doctor awoke before her.

She couldn't very well say, "I'm going out to horse around for a couple of hours—be back at eight." So instead she rushed to join Dr. Novak and find out what had him opening every cabinet and drawer.

"*Buenos días,*" Grace said, dressed and ready for the day.

"You're an early riser," he said. "That's good."

"Do you need help with whatever you're doing?"

"I'm done. I double-checked some of the inventory."

"We did that yesterday."

"I know. I'm pondering what I could give up if I have

56

to trade with the supply clerk in Mexicali for allergy kits."

"Is the money situation that bad? I thought the contest win earned you loads of income."

"My brother says I won over sixty thousand dollars."

"Wow. I'd like to see the photos that convinced women to fork out that much cash." She wondered if he wore *any* clothes in the poses but didn't dare ask.

"Don't get too excited. The funds are spoken for." He waited for that announcement to sink in. "And Chad's facing a stumbling block."

"It's one thing to cast a vote and another to pay?"

"No. The professor overseeing his thesis project wants him to formulate procedures to account for every donation. There's also some international snarl. He's working on it."

"Oh. He'll come through." Grace sensed the bond these brothers shared. Neither would break his word to the other.

"Chad estimates he'll deposit the first check in a few weeks. But a good portion of the prize is for an EKG machine and supplies and a new but low-grade X-ray machine and processor."

"That's fantastic. And so smart to use your good looks for something productive."

"Excuse me?"

Grace felt really, really dumb for making that remark.

"What would you consider an *un*productive use?"

Making women melt at your feet, she thought. "I didn't mean to say it like a compliment."

"What did you mean to say?"

That the contest tapped your best assets. "That the

contest was a brilliant idea." Grace suddenly felt hot. "There's something I've been wanting to do."

"What's that, Grace?" His warm gaze scanned her face.

Keep a safe distance from you, she thought. "Is it okay if I go for a walk along the seashore this morning? I've been dying to explore the beach since I arrived."

"Of course. In fact, a walk is just what I need before our lengthy drive. I'll join you."

He didn't ask. He invited himself. Not that she would have refused. But it would have been polite of him to ask.

Grace exited the clinic knowing that politeness was not one of Dr. Novak's attributes. That seemed to be a peculiarity of doctors of his kind. His confident type always assumed that they were wanted. It never occurred to them that a woman might not desire their company.

He led her down a dirt path through the residential area. They walked past shacks made of corrugated tin or palm fronds and the occasional house made of wood or adobe. Villagers starting their daily routines greeted them as they walked by.

"We can see the sunrise. It's a sight I never tire of," he said.

"You really treasure San Felipe, don't you?"

"When I originally visited, I thought it was Eden. The clean, uncrowded beach, the hospitality, the mountains for hiking, the cheap prices."

Grace sensed a hesitation. "But?"

"Now that I live here and care about these people, I see what's missing."

Grace glanced at a woman about her age feeding a

burro. Three small children played nearby. "It might not be Eden for them, but the villagers seem happy."

"They're hardworking, self-sufficient, and proud."

He could be describing himself, Grace thought.

"Not only do they need a fully functioning clinic with regular immunizations and checkups for the kids but, as you said, a school with decent textbooks and computers, a library, a gym or pool, and a school bus for field trips."

"Back home we take those things for granted."

"Here they're luxuries."

Ryan Novak fascinated her. His concern for the villagers appeared genuine.

They stepped past more homes and palm trees and finally faced the Sea of Cortez.

"What do you think of San Felipe's beach?"

"It's beautiful." The breeze carried to Grace the scent of Dr. Novak she'd gotten when she'd first met him. A pleasant, tropical sea breeze. She inhaled, thinking of him in his wet swim trunks. *Not again.* Immediately she reached up and yanked her ponytail.

"Are you okay?"

"Uh . . . my ponytail was a little tight."

The sun appeared on the horizon. The gold light spilled over the village. But the white, sandy beach in front of them, with the tranquil, splashing tide of the clear blue sea, cast a spell on her. Fishermen labored from their boats. As Grace stood in awe of the beauty before her, an adolescent boy and his father marched by carrying fishing poles and tackle boxes.

Dr. Novak spoke in Spanish to them.

"Everyone likes you," she said. She removed her shoes and walked on the wet sand. The tepid water rolled up to her ankles. Dr. Novak appeared to gaze quizzically at her legs and then threw off his own sandals.

"You've got a few fans yourself," he said.

"Not me."

"When you left the exam room after we stitched Jaime up, he confided his thoughts. Do you know what he said?"

" 'She looks like she's going to faint'?"

Dr. Novak laughed. "You showed confidence and bravery. Don't tell me you were feeling faint."

Not from the sight of blood. "Okay, I won't," she said. But thinking of Dr. Novak in those swim trunks and not much else brought up another question entirely. "You had no photo at all in the agency's portfolio on you. You could have used your contest photos."

"I suppose. But why would I want to do that?"

"Oh, I get it. I guess I don't blame you," she said, curious about who else might have come to San Felipe in search of the man of her dreams.

"You amaze me, Nurse Sinclair."

She took her gaze from the sea to him. "Why is that?"

He shook his head. "Jaime liked you. A lot. I think you're why he acted so brave."

"He's a brave boy. But I know Jaime calmed down a little the moment he saw you. He knew he was in reliable hands."

They walked in silence, listening to the waves lap at their ankles. A woman gathered shells in a woven basket.

"She makes jewelry and things out of the shells," Ryan pointed out. "The tourists love her creations."

"What's her name?"

"Mrs. Garza."

"Have you bought anything of hers?"

"I'm planning to buy my mom a necklace."

"Do you have any other women to buy for?" Grace hated when she voiced her nosy questions.

He arched his eyebrows. "That's a pretty personal question."

"Sorry. Sometimes my mouth operates before my brain kicks in."

"I'll answer if you'll answer a question for me."

Grace swallowed. She didn't really want to hear him talk about his love life. She especially didn't want to talk about hers.

"I don't have a woman in my life, nor do I want one. The last thing I need is an encumbrance."

Why am I not surprised? Grace thought. "Me either. One marriage was it for me," she said, feeling his gaze on her. "I have no interest whatsoever in any other man," she added.

"Great. My question is, do you want to learn to kayak?"

She stole a glance at him. "I'd love to. But the people here use the beach and the sea for their livelihood. Wouldn't it be a bit disrespectful to use it for something so frivolous?"

"This town depends on tourism too. The people who come to visit bring money into the town. They like to snorkel and kayak."

"In that case, yes."

"Great. We'll squeeze some fun into our schedule. But now it's time to collect Jaime and head to Mexicali."

Jaime talked the entire journey. He happily gave Grace a history lesson of the area. At last Mexicali's hospital came into view.

They followed Dr. Novak to the orthopedic clinic in the basement. The modernity of the hospital surprised Grace. Though a far cry from the state-of-the-art American hospital she'd come from, Grace had expected a rustic, under-equipped structure.

Professionals in scrubs or white uniforms hurried in the halls. Beepers beeped, and an intercom paged someone. Orderlies wheeled carts of supplies or gurneys with patients. Two doctors ran past the elevators and into the stairwell.

"Bring back memories?" Dr. Novak asked.

"Of the rat race I left behind?"

"It'll be difficult returning to it."

Was that a reminder that her position was only temporary? She could see herself in San Felipe longer than a year, but Dr. Novak had made his plans clear.

"You don't miss the bustle?" she asked.

"There's plenty of excitement in San Felipe. Jaime alone has created many exciting experiences."

"You see, I'm good for something," Jaime said.

"Today you're going to teach my nurse how to apply a cast."

Something tingled inside Grace when she heard him call her "my nurse."

First Jaime had an X-ray, and Dr. Novak consulted with the radiologist. They spoke in rapid Spanish. Next, they went down the hall to the cast room. It smelled like an arts-and-crafts class in an elementary school. Wet plaster.

Dr. Novak greeted the orthopedic technician and introduced Grace and Jaime. "I'd like you to instruct Grace as you proceed. Once I get my X-ray machine, we'll be able to apply casts for fractures that don't require surgery."

The pleasant technician explained every step to Grace. She had studied the technique in books, but seeing it done helped ease her concerns.

"First you wrap the Kerlix gauze around the arm, about one-quarter inch thick for cushioning," the technician said, as he wrapped. "Then the cloth dipped in the plaster goes over that."

"You try it," the man said. He handed her a strip of cloth. "Don't worry about dripping on the floor."

Grace's eyes widened.

"It's okay," Jaime said, his tone and expression full of trust. Grace smiled, attempting to show confidence for Jaime's benefit. She dunked the strip into the wet plaster, wrung it out, and smoothed it over the Kerlex gauze. The gooey, messy plaster hardened quickly. The tech handed her another piece of cloth. She saturated it, wrung it out, and applied it to Jaime's arm.

Grace repeated the procedure until the arm had a complete cast covering it.

Dr. Novak watched her closely the entire time. She felt his nearness.

"All done," the technician said. "He needs to wait for an hour, and then I'll give the cast a final check."

Grace beamed. She'd learned another new skill that nurses normally wouldn't have been taught.

"You did great," Dr. Novak said.

Grace nodded at Jaime. "Yes, you did," she said.

"The doctor speaks about you," Jaime said.

She glanced up to see Dr. Novak gazing at her.

"Oh. Thank you."

The technician glanced from one to the other and then at Jaime.

Jaime raised his eyebrows repeatedly, relaying a silent message to the technician. He got it.

"That's enough, you little scamp," Novak said. "We've got more stops before we head home. Wait here. We'll be back." Dr. Novak thanked the technician, and he and Grace left. "Central Supply is down the hall."

The young woman behind the desk lit up when she saw Dr. Novak. She gushed all over him, and another woman in scrubs joined in. The pair completely ignored Grace.

He placed his order form on the counter, and the two nearly fought over it.

Grace laughed.

"What's so funny?" Ryan asked.

"Doctor, you didn't need to bring items to trade. Next time just bring one of your contest photos, and these two will give you anything you need."

"I don't want to get anyone fired." He wasn't amused. "Whatever you do, don't mention the contest to them."

"Isn't that why they're your fans?"

"No. They were like this before the Web site ever went up."

Grace chuckled. "You should tell them. I'm sure they'd vote for you."

He flung a warning glance her way.

As it turned out, La Clínica Pediátrica had a positive credit balance, though not by much.

"Gracias, señoritas." Dr. Novak thanked the ladies as he took his allergy kits and other supplies.

"Adiós!" They swooned one more time.

"You only have one hundred and twenty dollars left in your account?" Grace asked, when they reached the hall.

"I'm expecting a foundation grant allotment in a week."

"And if it's delayed?"

"Barring any catastrophes, we should be okay for two weeks."

"You like living on the edge."

"It's not very secure, I know. My parents flip out over my management style."

"They don't approve of just-in-time budgeting?"

He laughed. "Not the Novaks. They like having their business ventures well funded, as well as a budget for emergencies."

"Contingency funds are a necessity for any start-up," she said. "Even a nonprofit."

"How do you know that?"

"My family has its share of businesspeople."

They collected Jaime, waited for the technician's final check, and hit the road.

"I'd like to hear more about your family," he said.

"Why not? It's a long drive to San Felipe." Grace adored her parents and sister. She'd actually had a happy life before her doctor-husband turned it upside down. She'd leave that part out.

Grace hadn't realized she'd chattered so much until she noticed that Jaime had fallen asleep. "I talk too much."

"It's only too much if you're dull. You're interesting."

Compared to his life, hers bordered between lackluster and excruciatingly boring.

"It sounds like you and your sister are close. Is she older or younger than you?"

"Amber's two years older. We had a lot of fun growing up. Our favorite thing to do when we were little was perform in plays for our parents and other relatives. We'd create short productions with homemade costumes, and everyone was certain we would become movie stars. Now she's a successful interior designer and married to a man who adores her."

Dr. Novak chuckled. "I can *almost* see you as a drama queen."

Grace turned to glance at him. "Humph. I'll take that as a compliment. We loved the high drama scenes."

"Oh, I bet you had legions of adoring fans."

Grace laughed as she watched him drive. "I'd like to know more about what persuades a man to pack up everything and move to an impoverished foreign village where he's sure to work harder and earn much less than if he stayed home."

"I told you what brought me here," he said.

"But what made you stay?"

"I wanted to make a difference."

He had indeed already done that. "You're only one person, and you've accomplished so much."

"That's what I set out to do."

"There's more to it, though. Something drove you to volunteer for the Doctors Without Borders assignment in the first place." She studied his profile. He could have applied his determination to any goal, in any hospital. Yet he'd chosen this path. He must have set out to be a hero a long time ago.

"Is it so important to you that I gave up a high-paying career for a destitute lifestyle?" He tightened his grip on the steering wheel.

"It's noteworthy that you're that committed. I've never met anyone like you." She shouldn't have revealed that last sentence. Grace fiddled with her hands in her lap. "Besides, if money were a big deal to me, do you think I would have accepted this job?"

He exhaled. He drove in silence for a few moments and relaxed.

"At medical school I saw a memorial plaque for a doctor. It read that he was blessed with skilled hands, which he used to comfort his patients, teach his students, and love his family. And that he would never be forgotten." Novak shrugged. "I read it every day, and it inspired me. I decided then that that was the life I wanted."

His admission stunned Grace. She hadn't expected such a deeply personal reply.

"Nothing in that plaque mentioned money, fame, or a fancy practice. Just dedication and love," he said.

Grace turned away so he couldn't see her moist eyes. Maybe all doctors *weren't* the same. She cleared her throat.

"That's an amazing goal," she said quietly. Dr. Ryan Novak stood out from the pack in more ways than one. He differed from her husband in the dedication aspect, yet her intuition still warned her to stay on her guard. *Remember why you're here, Grace. Stop being so gullible for poignant words.* She loathed that trait in herself.

The Jeep bumped over something in the road, and his leg brushed against hers. It happened inadvertently, she knew, but that did not deter her sudden awareness of him. His raw sex appeal pervaded her senses, plagued her. It was his shorts, she decided. If only the man could wear pants!

"Oh, look!" Grace shouted, purposely awaking Jaime. Feeling her cheeks flush, she refused to look at Dr. Novak.

"What is it?" Jaime said.

"Um . . . a coyote."

The boy laughed. "Coyotes do not come out in the daylight," Jaime said. With renewed energy he chatted endlessly about Baja California wildlife.

Somehow Grace managed not to peek at Dr. Novak's legs the rest of the trip. But the more she tried to ignore Dr. Novak, the more she noticed about him. She loathed this trait in herself too. Whatever it was. She should get out of the Jeep right now and take her chances with the coyotes.

Finally they reached San Felipe. Dr. Novak helped Jaime out of the Jeep. "See me in three days so I can check those sutures and the cast."

"Sí, Doctor." The boy thanked them and went home.

Now Grace had to get through the night—the long night—with Dr. Novak alone.

"Let's eat," he said, oblivious to her distress.

Chapter Six

Dr. Novak appeared in the doorway to his office. "There'll be a quiz when I return," he said.

Grace glanced up from the papers strewn about his desk. He leaned on the door frame, arms crossed. His scent hit her then. That tantalizing blend of soap and sea and aftershave. He'd just showered, and his damp hair curled at his brow and temples. Wearing another absurd shirt and ultrabright lime shorts with flip-flops, he gazed at her with green eyes that glimmered.

"I'll do my best," she said, swallowing the lump that formed in her throat. Only an overconfident personality could pull off that outfit. Where did the man shop for his clothes? Was there a bargain store for neon apparel in this part of Mexico?

He followed her gaze to his shorts. "A factory outlet in Guadalupe. I'll take you there sometime."

"I can't wait," she said with a smile.

He remained relaxed as he observed her. "You look good behind my desk."

"You mean working, while you're off having fun?"

He chuckled. "That must be it." He straightened. "Have everything you need?"

No. Not everything. She cleared her throat. "Yes."

He placed a Duke University baseball cap on his head.

Those curls would beguile any living woman. Except her. She was immune to his charisma. "Why wear a hat at night? Or shouldn't I ask?"

"It's my good-luck hat."

"Of course."

"Wish me luck." He turned and strode down the hallway.

Only when Grace heard the clinic door close did she exhale. She lifted a folder and fanned herself and wished for the old geezer boss she'd thought she might be getting. Things would be much simpler and less stressful . . . and certainly less colorful. She gathered up the papers she'd organized into piles and put each stack into a folder: one for *Applications Denied,* one for each of the two approved grants, one labeled *Government Records,* one for *Clinic Budget,* one for *Grant Possibilities,* and one marked *Miscellaneous Info.* She found one empty folder marked *Mailing List.*

It occurred to her that filing was the only chore the perfect doctor neglected. A totally forgivable offense.

Now that she'd sorted the avalanche of papers on his desk, she opened the *Applications Denied* folder. The inch-thick file had four proposals inside. She might as well read them, she decided. Perhaps they could be strengthened, and she could reapply.

An hour later she'd read the proposals. They were identical to the ones sent to the other two organizations.

The budget section perplexed Grace. There had to be an error. Locating the *Clinic Budget* folder, she studied the spreadsheet inside.

"Holy cow. It's not an error." She glanced at the supporting documents inside the folder. "Dr. Novak only gives himself a daily salary of one dollar!"

How can he support himself on that? she wondered. Volunteering for philanthropic stints was one thing, but La Clínica Pediátrica was clearly not a short-term assignment for him. "You're more chivalrous than I thought," she said aloud, somehow knowing that Dr. Novak hadn't shared this secret with any of the villagers. Surely Carmen would have boasted about it.

"They adore you enough," she said to his photo on the wall. Grace rose to get a closer look at the wall of photographs. Beside shots of a younger, perhaps college-age Ryan Novak were more recent shots of him with some of the villagers. He smiled in all of them. *Now here's a man who doesn't seem to have any regrets, a man who lives life to the fullest.* As Grace gawked at a close-up of him, something lurched in her stomach. His green eyes sparkled back at her, as they had many times in person.

What kind of a woman could keep a man like him happy? Not herself, that was for sure. Grace couldn't even handle an ordinary man. She was no match for one as extraordinary as Dr. Novak. Good thing she had no personal interest in him!

Still, she wondered if he preferred strong, challenging types or quiet, agreeable women. Perhaps, like her husband, Dr. Novak didn't limit himself to any one type.

The heaviness she often felt lately in her chest returned. Her husband would have taken a couple of hours to "make amends" with Mandy too. And he'd return crowing about her as Novak had. The heaviness deepened. She had wanted Ryan Novak to be a good guy. She had wanted to believe that at least one doctor in the world existed who didn't run around breaking women's hearts.

Whatever. She couldn't let the man's personal habits affect their working relationship.

Reverting to the budget file, Grace continued unraveling the mystery of Dr. Novak's equipment acquisitions. Somehow he'd found hospitals ready to surplus obsolete items and had purchased them for pennies on the dollar. The delivery logistics seemed to simulate those of covert military strategists.

One sheet of paper had a diagram and several names and cities on the reverse side of it. Some names had been crossed off. This "invoice" started in San Francisco with a surgical ceiling light and four wheelchairs, stopped in Monterey for a medicine cabinet, and went on to Puerto Catarina, Mexico, to drop off the wheelchairs and pick up two surgical-steel rolling trays.

Another "invoice" showed shipment by sea for oxygen equipment. The ship's name, *Fancy Pants,* and a scribbled name, *Larry,* on the bottom informed Grace that a traditional shipping firm had not been used. A Post-it note message said, *Larry and Linda vacation in Cabo San Lucas every other year.*

From what she could tell, Dr. Novak had called in every favor ever owed him by friends in the hospital business. But as she read the pages, her curiosity grew. And her admiration for him swelled. Dr. Novak had launched a high-tech international barter system.

Suddenly Grace had questions. Maybe she could get some answers. She shut off the lights and locked the front door. *Oops.* Now she'd need his key to get back in. *Oh, well.* She'd figure that out later.

Inside the cantina, six stoic-faced men sat at a round table. None glanced from his poker hand to greet her.

"Hi, Grace," Dr. Novak said, without looking up from his cards.

"Hi, yourself." She wondered how he knew she had entered.

"Graciela, *venga.*" *Come this way,* Carmen said.

Grace passed the table. She recognized Dr. Novak, Poncho, and Gabriel but not the other three men playing or the few who watched.

"It looks serious," she said to Carmen, noticing the large mound of chips at stake.

"The ante's ten American dollars."

"Is that all?" Grace relaxed.

"That's *mucho dinero*," Carmen said.

"Yes, it is," Grace corrected herself. "With all those chips, I worried it was much more."

The conversation picked up among the men, if you could call grunts and one-syllable words *conversation.* Then came the clink of chips before the players smacked down their cards. Only the winner, Poncho, revealed his hand. The group grew boisterous, chatting in Spanish.

Grace smiled at how at-home Dr. Novak looked in this scenario. Hanging out in a Mexican cantina, playing poker with the locals, drinking Dos Equis beer, and wearing tourist attire. She forced her gaze up from his once-again bare legs. If those legions of fans could see him like this, they'd never stop chasing him.

"You have to put up with this every week?" Grace asked Carmen.

"They play only once or twice a month. I don't mind."

"Gabriel's a lucky man." Grace focused her attention on the tortillas Carmen was making. The savory aroma permeated her senses. "Could you teach me how to cook?" Grace sat on a stool.

Benita passed with a tray of dirty dishes. She and Carmen exchanged glances. They both grinned.

"If it's not too much trouble," Grace added.

"No trouble," Carmen said.

"I can help. I know all the doctor's favorite dishes," Benita said.

Grace jumped off the stool a little too eagerly. "When can we start?"

"Right now." Carmen pulled Grace over. "Wash up in the sink. You can start with tortillas."

Grace rolled up her sleeves and watched Carmen use the rolling pin to flatten the *masa*. Then Carmen handled the *masa* much like a pizza maker stretching his dough. Another pass with the rolling pin and—*olé!*—a perfect tortilla.

"That looks easy," Grace said. But even following Carmen's precise example, her tortillas came out in the shape of Texas.

Carmen demonstrated again. Grace tried again. This time the tortilla almost resembled a rectangle. "Why isn't it working?"

"It just takes practice," Carmen comforted her.

"My first tortillas came out like that too," Benita said.

"Really? How old were you?" Grace pummeled the *masa* with the rolling pin.

"Five."

Grace realized Benita had thought her words were constructive; otherwise she might have found a second use for the rolling pin.

She kept trying. Finally she made a circular tortilla. "Hey, look! It's round." Grace proudly held it up. "Almost."

Benita and Carmen applauded for her.

"Put it on the burner." Carmen slapped it onto a flat skillet. "Start the next one, but don't forget to flip this one over or it will burn."

Grace nodded. She worked the dough while keeping an eye on the cooking tortilla. She successfully made the flip. Seconds later, she carefully removed it and added the next one. "I did it!"

Grace glanced up to find Benita cleaning off a table and Carmen taking the order at another. Yet she felt someone staring. She turned and caught Dr. Novak's warm, lingering gaze on her. The sultry expression in his eyes made the room spin. *Is that look for me?* Grace didn't want him looking at her like that.

"That's my girl," he mouthed.

She stood frozen. She had to have misread his lips. Maybe he'd mouthed, *get me chips,* or *watch the grill.* Just then Grace inhaled smoke.

At the same moment she heard Carmen's voice, Grace saw Dr. Novak's expression transform into alarm. She coughed and glanced at the skillet. Her tortilla was charred, with a thick cloud billowing above the stove.

"Uh-oh!" She panicked.

Carmen abruptly turned off the burner and fanned the stove with her white dish towel. Well, if Grace hadn't garnered every customer's attention by now, the smoke signals Carmen was sending certainly would. Benita flipped the hood fan on and hacked.

Grace wanted to disappear. Until she heard laughter. Uninhibited, prolonged laughter . . . from several men. Her humiliation evolved into annoyance. Especially toward the doctor, who seemed to laugh the loudest.

"I'm sorry, Carmen. Did I damage anything?"

"No. Just a tortilla."

More laughter.

Grace eyed the rolling pin. Finally the smoke reached the poker table, and the laughing men started to cough. Gabriel hurriedly opened the cantina's doors.

Please don't let my foolishness ruin everyone's dinner. But the breeze worked well, quickly dissipating the smoke. Gabriel and Carmen reassured the patrons. Grace slipped out the back door.

The smoke must have gotten to her brain, making her imagine the doctor had looked at her as if she were special. That idea was as ridiculous as her kitchen stunt.

A noise caught her attention. It came from the side of the building. Grace followed the noise—a person retching.

"Benita!" Grace ran to her side. "Is it the smoke?"

Benita shook her head.

"I'll get the doctor."

Benita clamped a hand on Grace's wrist. "No."

She waited until Benita stopped retching. "What is it?"

"I . . . I've got the flu."

Grace checked her forehead. Cool and clammy, not

feverish, but her face had paled. "Why didn't you stay home?"

"I need to work." Benita shrugged. "My body aches, and I have a headache." She thought for a moment. "And chills."

Those *were* flu symptoms. "Since when?"

"Since yesterday. This is my first nausea, though."

Grace felt guilty that the smoke had likely provoked it. "You need rest. I'll help Carmen with the cleanup."

"That's my job."

"Not tonight. Go home."

Benita hesitated.

"It's only—what . . . another hour?" Grace said.

"You need rest too." Benita looked weak.

"After the hassle I caused, I would sleep better knowing I helped clean," Grace said earnestly.

"*Bueno,* you win."

"Win what?" Dr. Novak asked, suddenly at Grace's side.

Grace scowled at him. "Darn, I left the rolling pin inside."

Benita chuckled as she brushed past him, with Grace on her heels.

"Hey, what did I do?" he asked.

Chapter Seven

Come on, Grace. Don't you ever laugh at yourself?"

"You did sufficient laughing for both of us."

"Well, it was funny. Admit it."

She'd given him the cold shoulder since last night, providing him the opportunity to pursue her back to the clinic building and ask for her forgiveness. Ryan rather enjoyed following Grace. He'd discovered some interesting things about her. She had the ability to walk very fast, witty quips rolled off her tongue, and she made an adorable face when she forced herself to scowl.

"At least let me make it up to you."

"You agree to the flogging?"

"No." He held in his smile. "Besides, this is Mexico. It's called *la zurra.*"

"To show your remorse, let me *zurrar* you."

She made it sound appealing. "Change into your bathing suit. We're going out to sea."

Her eyes brightened. "But we have work . . ."

"Paperwork. It can wait. You've earned some time off." He happily postponed his least favorite task.

Smiling, she said, "Give me two minutes."

He watched her hurry down the hallway. Now he knew her weakness. The sea.

Ryan changed in thirty seconds. When Grace reappeared, she took his breath away with her loveliness. He'd never known that a modest, one-piece bathing suit could look so darn alluring. Even with a shirt cover-up her curves tempted him. And her legs. He had to drag his gaze away from her legs.

She's your employee, he reminded himself. *A widow. She's off-limits.*

"You're wearing those trunks," Grace blurted. Her cheeks reddened, rousing his interest. What had she expected?

"I usually wear these when I swim." He tossed a towel at her. "Unless I swim nude."

He heard her soft gasp. He considered offering her a skinny-dip, but he was supposed to be begging forgiveness, not getting into further trouble.

The warm morning sun shone down on the white, glittering beach. As Grace and Ryan walked, a handful of small boats dotted the sea with their experienced fishermen casting their nets. He inhaled the refreshing sea air.

"I wish I could bottle that scent," he said.

"That would be remarkable, to bottle pleasant memories," she said wistfully.

He glanced at Grace, her hair shining from the sun's light, wondering what she would think of his wanting to bottle *her* scent. *Don't go there.* Even if she weren't his nurse, Grace was a grieving widow. *Show some respect. Leave her alone.*

"For someone who loves the sea so much, you rarely seem to come out to enjoy it," she said.

"But I know it's here, and I glimpse it from the clinic."

"You gave me the bedroom with the view," she said, observing him. "When I look out the window, it always makes me yearn to come down here."

Yet she doesn't act on her yearning, he noted. What would make Grace loosen up? Not that he wanted a loose nurse.

"And here we are," he said. He gestured at a shack up ahead. "We can rent what we need from Chico."

She walked alongside him. The sand crunched beneath his flip-flops and her sandals. Ryan fought the urge to take her hand. He did not understand why he felt like a high schooler around Grace. He obviously needed to socialize more. When had he last kissed a woman? Eons ago. That explained why he fantasized so much about Grace. It wasn't like him to get distracted. Or perhaps it had to do with her proximity and nothing more. Now that he'd analyzed it, he relaxed. All he had to do was see other women. He ignored the coil in his gut.

Grace raced her kayak, keeping up with Dr. Novak. At first he'd tried to outmaneuver her; now he tried to outlast her.

"I'm not giving up!" she called out. She felt alive, invigorated.

"You'll eat your words." He laughed, paddling harder. "I'm a champion kayaker."

"Former champion!" she shouted. "Admit you've met your match!" Every muscle in her body burned, but she welcomed the confirmation that she was a living person. For too long she'd been numb—and dormant. The sea air, the laughter, the vigorous activity revitalized her spirit.

"Never!" He gained momentum.

"Ha!" was all she could muster. Never had anyone challenged her in every way, as Ryan Novak had, forcing her to step it up. Paddling with every ounce of strength, she'd caught up to him. She squealed, trying to pass his kayak. He didn't let her. So much for chivalry.

"Never, ever!"

His wide smile caused her heart to somersault. The doctor had single-handedly resuscitated her soul. And gawking at his flexing muscles all morning had awakened other parts of her that had been deadened too. But she didn't want to admit it.

Grace noticed the gleam of perspiration on his chest. And now his forehead. Finally. How much longer could he last?

"Give up yet?" he taunted, not breaking his stride.

"No!"

Her body ached. She'd pay for her stubbornness the rest of the week.

One by one, the fishing boats had come in. Only a lone fisherman remained at sea.

"It's lunchtime," he shouted. "Aren't you hungry?"

"Yes," she admitted.

"How about a truce?"

Her competitive nature fired up. "That's as bad as a tie!"

He laughed. "Okay, whoever reaches that buoy first."

Grace didn't answer. She sped off.

He grunted alongside her, keeping pace with her kayak. Grace summoned everything she had left, focusing on the buoy, but she barely moved ahead of him. The tip of his kayak came nearly flush with hers, and they reached the buoy at the same instant.

"It's a tie!" He raised his paddle in the air, hooting as if in victory.

She sat winded with her paddle across her lap. Their kayaks glided to a stop. Grace tried to appear annoyed, but she couldn't keep her smile from spreading.

"What a workout." His eyes gleamed at her.

"That was just a warm-up," she said.

As he chuckled, he dipped his hand into the sea and splashed water on himself. "And you said you weren't athletic."

They drifted as their bodies adjusted, and Grace would have liked to float out there all afternoon. Though lunchtime beckoned, she didn't think she had the energy to lift a fork. Besides, what better way to spend the morning than lazily observing Ryan Novak splash water over his toned muscles?

"A *centavo* for your thoughts," he said.

"I love it here," she said, scooping up a handful of the sea to wet her face. Too bad it wasn't ice water.

"Then you're not mad at me anymore?"

Grace had forgotten. "No. You're off the hook."

He breathed a melodramatic sigh of relief. "So, why'd you barge into the cantina last night?"

"I didn't barge in. I had questions."

"You planned on interrupting my poker game for questions?"

"I thought you might take a break."

"A break during poker?"

Who knew? "How did you locate surplus hospital equipment? And the coordination . . . that's like a full-time job in itself."

"Connections."

It wasn't *that* easy. She waited.

"I had a job during breaks at med school. One of those gofer kind of jobs. You know—delivery, cleaning, moving furniture."

Grace tried to concentrate on his words and not the drops of water slipping down his chest and arms. Good thing his legs were hidden from her view.

"I found out the school got grants for some new equipment every year, and whatever items they purchased, the old stuff got sold as surplus. Most of the time the old items worked fine; they just wanted newer, improved models."

"So you looked into that when you graduated from your residency."

"Exactly. And I asked colleagues to call their alma maters and get me equipment the same way. But an X-ray machine and processor have been hard to come by."

Grace guessed that if Dr. Novak had asked female colleagues, he'd have his X-ray machine in no time. What woman could resist going the extra mile for him?

"You used your grant money for the supplies and medicines. But why don't you give yourself a salary?" she asked.

"It was a negotiating chip with Poncho. It got him to

lower the rent to one dollar a month for the first eighteen months."

So Poncho was a saint too. "That's wonderful, but how can you live on one dollar a day?"

"I have a roof over my head, and my living expenses are low. I trade for anything I need."

"Who owns *Fancy Pants?*"

He grinned. "Friends of my parents. You found one of my invoices."

"They came all the way from the States as a favor?"

"They came for a vacation. I showed them a good time too."

"I think we should briefly mention some of those acquisitions in future grant proposals," she said.

His skin had tanned nicely under the sun's rays, Grace noticed. Then her gaze caught something behind him. A fishing boat drifting, but the fisherman wasn't in sight.

"Something's wrong." Grace paddled toward the boat. Dr. Novak reached it first.

"Señor! Hola, señor." He grabbed the narrow boat.

The man was slumped over, unresponsive. "Hold the boat still," Dr. Novak said, climbing out of his kayak and leaping onto the fishing vessel. It nearly flipped over. He quickly assessed the unconscious man.

"It's Mr. Garza. I don't feel a pulse." He bent and listened to the man's chest. "He's not breathing!"

"He's in cardiac arrest." The man's pale face alarmed her. How long had he been in apnea? "Let me do the CPR."

Dr. Novak had begun the rescue breathing, but the one-person boat tilted perilously with his weight. "I can't give effective compressions."

"I know. Get out." She held on to the fishing boat. "Hurry."

His kayak had drifted, so he jumped into the sea. Grace stood carefully. Her thighs protested. Just balancing herself used up energy and had her aching muscles quivering.

Holding the rail of the boat, she stepped in. It tilted but not as dangerously as it had under Ryan's weight. Grace made sure Señor Garza's torso lay flat with nothing beneath him to prevent a complete chest compression.

She began CPR. Her body went into automatic mode. Two breaths, thirty compressions. Two breaths, thirty compressions.

"How are you doing, Grace?"

She paused to check Mr. Garza's carotid pulse and breathing. "Nothing," she said, continuing the CPR. The confines of the fishing boat made her kneel in an awkward position for CPR. Señor Garza had been sitting up when they raced past him. He must not have been unconscious for more than a few minutes. "Come on, Señor Garza. Breathe." The boat wobbled with her movements.

Grace heard paddling and felt motion. She glanced up during the compressions. Dr. Novak had tied a rope from her kayak to the fishing vessel and was towing them to shore.

"Are you okay?" he called out.

Grace paused, placing two fingers on Señor Garza's neck. "No response!" She proceeded. Two breaths, thirty compressions. Two breaths, thirty compressions. She rocked the boat more than she liked when she made the switch from breathing to compressing his sternum. Was she giving effective compressions with the bobbing of the boat?

"Hang on, Grace. We're almost there!"

Two breaths, thirty compressions. Grace paused again. This time she got a carotid pulse. "Circulation restored!" But still no breathing. She continued the mouth-to-mouth, adjusting her count.

"Good job!"

Grace heard a gurgling sound and angled Garza's head away from her, listening. He vomited.

"Brace yourself!" Dr. Novak called.

The boat bumped roughly against the shore. Chico and some other villagers had gathered. *"Qué pasa?"*

Frenzied dialogue in Spanish.

"Help me get him to *la clínica*," Dr. Novak shouted. Everyone moved into action. Except Grace.

"He vomited. His breathing may have restarted," she said. "I didn't get to check it."

"I'll take care of him," he said.

The villagers hoisted Garza to shoulder level and marched off at a trot.

Her alert mind registered everything. It was her body that shut down. An adrenaline rush on the fisherman's boat had kept her going, but that had run out. She felt as if she'd been through a full cycle in a dryer. Or in the ring with a prize fighter. One throbbing lump of useless tissue. Her muscles didn't function; she couldn't move if she had to. "Go on. I'll catch up."

Dr. Novak mumbled something that sounded like cursing; then he lifted her out of the boat. He carried her up the hill to the clinic. She sank into his arms, reveling in the smell of the sea on his skin and the feel of his chest against her cheek. She'd really like to bottle *this* memory.

Chapter Eight

Grace awoke to the sound of soft murmurs. Her body ached like the devil.

"I'm sure she's hungry, but right now she's exhausted," Dr. Novak whispered.

"You have grown rather protective of her," a woman said.

"Who, me?" Grace said. "I'm starving."

"Graciela!" Carmen shouted. She and Dr. Novak appeared at her side.

Where was she?

"Grace, how are you?" Ryan lifted her hand in his.

Grace fought past the fog of fatigue. "Why are you taking my pulse?" Disappointment crept into her voice. "I thought you were holding my hand."

Carmen made an odd noise.

Grace sat up, fully alert. As she helped her sit, Carmen smiled widely.

"Why do I have an IV going?"

"You were dehydrated. You had quite a morning."

It all rushed back. "Señor Garza?"

"You revived him. We brought him here for treatment. I kept him stable until the medevac chopper airlifted him to Mexicali."

CPR. The fishing boat. It had worked.

"You're phenomenal, Grace," he said.

"You would've done the same thing."

"I couldn't."

"You brought us back. You paddled the weight of two people and a fishing boat and a kayak," she said.

"Two kayaks," Carmen said proudly.

Grace smiled at Carmen. Every muscle in Grace screamed with soreness. She rubbed her arms.

"I gave you some ibuprofen in here," Dr. Novak said, wiggling the bag of D5W. "If you need something stronger . . ."

"I'm fine. When will we hear how Señor Garza's doing?"

"A couple of hours."

"How long did I sleep?"

"Barely ninety minutes."

The door of the clinic opened, and voices sounded.

"I will see who it is," Carmen said, leaving the two of them alone.

"Well, we've got patients who need this room. Back to work," Grace said, swinging her legs off the exam table and realizing with a shock that she wore only a paper gown!

Her cheeks flushed.

Who had undressed her? "Where's my bathing suit?"

Ryan watched her with a gleam in his eye. "It was still wet."

Grace wanted to hide. The skimpy gown stopped above the knee. Too much of her felt exposed. She pulled on the hem, which caused his gaze to follow her hands.

"I'm a doctor," he said, in a silky tone.

"You took advantage of my exhaustion!"

Carmen burst in. "What's the matter, Graciela?"

"I need my clothes."

"I'd like you to go to bed," Dr. Novak said.

"Go take a hike," Grace shot back, expertly removing her IV.

Carmen bent and retrieved clothing from the shelf below the exam table. "*El doctor* asked me to get you a change of clothes before I removed your swimsuit."

Grace felt completely mortified. She glanced at Dr. Novak, and he grinned innocently at her.

"Grace's modesty is charming. But she's forgotten I've seen her in a bathing suit." He winked and exited the room.

Ryan evaluated the patient solo, trying to shake thoughts of Grace out of his head. He didn't know why he had teased her. He had purposely misled her. All he knew was that his pulse had raced as he'd glimpsed her shapely legs protruding from the paper gown. And he knew she wore nothing underneath that gown. He'd felt hot and bothered. Maybe he'd wanted her to experience the heat too.

For a moment they had both shared the same mental image: that of him undressing her.

Twice today he'd wanted to pull Grace into his arms and kiss her. Not a cordial kiss either, but a visceral, profound kiss that went on and on. He suddenly craved her kisses.

But he had no right to them. He had to back off, stop being so obvious about his attraction to her. He needed to focus. Even if she weren't a widow, he couldn't pursue an affair with Grace.

At least ten things went through his head of what made a romp with her a bad idea. *No more fantasizing!*

"What is my problem, Doctor?"

His patient's voice nudged him back to the present.

"It's heartburn. I'll give you some chewable tablets." Ryan wheeled his chair to a supply drawer and withdrew a packet of antacid tablets. "I'm afraid you'll have to cut back on your wife's spicy cooking."

"Until when?"

"Just cut back. We'll watch what happens for two weeks. Chew the tablets for the pain and discomfort, but no more than three times a day. From what you've told me and from your symptoms, a permanent change to your diet may be necessary."

"What will I eat?"

"Ask your wife to reduce the spiciness of your meals. I'm hoping that's all that's needed."

"But I like hot food."

"I don't want you to burn a hole through your stomach. Do you?"

"Ouch." His patient frowned as he rubbed his abdomen.

"Come on. I'll tell her." Ryan rose, and pain shot through his own body. He grimaced.

"Doctor?"

Ryan held up a finger to his lips. "Shh." He hurt all over, but he sure as hell wasn't about to complain. If Grace could bear it, so could he.

As he opened the door, Grace's voice reached him. She spoke amicably with the patient's wife. The two men stepped into the waiting room, and Ryan's gaze slammed into Grace's. Expectation crackled in the air. Her lips parted. And Ryan thought about kissing her again.

"The doctor says I need to change my diet," the patient said.

His wife seemed baffled. *"Qué?"*

Ryan explained, aware that Grace watched him closely.

At last the couple left, agreeing to alter their meals.

Grace fiddled with the schedule. "We have four appointments left."

"Why don't you go get lunch? I can manage," he said.

For an instant, Grace looked hurt. But she promptly masked it.

"Providing no one unexpected pops in. Or anyone is worse off than when they made the appointment. Or an emergency that requires your attention occurs."

Or anything that required him to exert his sore muscles.

She laughed. "It's all right. I'd rather wait until dinner."

Did she know what her laugh did to his insides? *Damn. Knock it off, Novak!* He glanced at his watch. Two hours. "Same with me. I've progressed beyond hunger too." For food anyway. He scribbled notes in his heartburn patient's chart.

"Why did you deliberately embarrass me before?" she asked.

"It seemed like a good idea at the time," he said casually, not looking up from the chart.

"You're lucky I didn't slap you."

Ryan rubbed his cheek. "I didn't know you were so fierce."

"Now you know," she said.

"I learn something new about you every day." He still hadn't apologized. Grace would easily recognize that he didn't mean it. She already knew him far too well.

He closed the patient's records.

They both heard the heavy but quick footsteps on the porch.

Poncho barged in. *"Hola!"*

"Come in," Ryan said, relieved to have the distraction.

"We heard about your heroics this morning," Poncho said in his booming voice. "Petra insists you come to the ranch for dinner tonight." He leaned on the desk. "If you refuse, I will be in *mucho* trouble." He glanced at Grace. "How do you say . . . ah . . . in the doghouse."

"Oh, my," she said.

"We can't let that happen," Ryan said.

"What time should we come?" Grace asked.

"Six. My wife and I are eager to hear your story."

The man departed just as boisterously as he had entered.

The remainder of the afternoon passed quickly, with two pediatric drop-ins between the scheduled patients. One with an ear infection, the other for a diaper rash.

After the last patient left, Grace tallied up the supplies used and completed a reordering form.

"I'll check on Señor Garza from my office." Ryan withdrew the cell phone from his pocket. "You can have the shower first."

"Thanks. I'll take it."

As Grace marched away, Ryan forced his brain not to think of her in the shower. When his turn came, he'd take an icy cold rinse.

That evening Dr. Novak drove the Jeep through an arched gateway with an overhanging sign.

"La Hacienda de Esperanza," Grace read aloud.

"Ranch of Hope," he said.

"Do they have children?" Grace asked.

"Five. But they're all grown. They have lots of grand-children."

They were met at the door by a beautiful, slender Mexican woman, Petra, and Poncho. Petra shooed away the housemaid and graciously welcomed them into her home.

"I am so happy to finally meet you, Grace," Petra said with an exotic accent. She led them into a beautifully decorated parlor. The housemaid waited nearby. "What would you like to drink?" Petra asked.

Grace noticed Petra had a small glass of ruby liquid on the polished coffee table beside her. "I'll have whatever you're drinking," she said.

Everyone looked at Dr. Novak. *"Un Dos Equis, por favor."*

The housemaid hurried away.

The typically unabashed Poncho gentled near Petra, giving her the center stage. "It's only the four of us tonight. My wife wanted you to have a quiet evening after all your excitement."

"Before I leap into questions about your adventure

this morning, I must ask how Señor Garza is," Petra said.

"He's responding well to treatment. He suffered a low-grade heart attack. Luckily Grace discovered him when she did," Dr. Novak said.

"Thank God," Petra agreed, squeezing Grace's hand with both of hers.

The contact reassured Grace—until she spotted Petra's huge diamond ring. The wedding set had glittering diamonds across the band and on either side of the filigree setting that housed the largest stone. Grace's wedding ring had consisted of a plain, thin gold band.

Had it only been one month since Grace had flushed that band down the toilet?

She felt Dr. Novak's curious gaze on her. The housemaid returned with their drinks.

"A toast," Petra said. "To Señor Garza's speedy recovery." They clinked their glasses. "And to Grace's bravery."

"Dr. Novak is the one who kept him alive," Grace said.

"And to Dr. Novak," Petra added.

More clinking glasses.

The smooth liquid warmed Grace, and she relaxed.

"Tell me all about it," Petra said.

They chatted, ate dinner, and laughed for hours.

The entire evening Poncho doted on Petra. He pulled the chair out for her when she sat. He listened to her talk with genuine interest. He touched her often—a squeeze to her shoulder, a kiss on the temple. He clearly adored and respected his wife after more than thirty years of marriage.

Grace realized her husband had never behaved that

way, not even on their honeymoon. He had been needy and more concerned about his comfort than hers. Sure, he'd had his romantic moments, but in retrospect that was a means for him to get what he wanted. Grace would have enjoyed a doting husband.

She stole a glance at Dr. Novak, wondering what sort of a husband he would make.

But he surprised her by his potent observation of *her*. How long had he been studying her? Had Poncho or Petra noticed? His gaze did not abruptly turn away; rather, it skimmed intimately over her, as if he was just now discovering his awareness of her as a woman.

Her nerves twisted in turmoil. She'd worn a short black dress that rested mid-thigh when she sat. She hadn't given much thought to the dress earlier—it being the only nice dress in her wardrobe. Now, with Dr. Novak's eyes gleaming, she was having second thoughts. He smiled at her.

Rattled and resisting the urge to grab a sofa pillow and cover herself, she sipped her drink and focused on Petra.

For her part, Petra laughed at Poncho's jokes, flirted with him, and made sure he had what he needed, whether a fresh drink or more food or a comfortable place to sit. Petra spoke highly of her husband with never a put-down, not even jokingly.

Grace was unaccustomed to such a display of affection. Not with her parents and certainly not in her own marriage. Petra and Poncho were clearly very much in love. They had a quiet, solid marriage.

Sitting in their parlor after dinner, Grace compared them to Gabriel and Carmen. The latter couple seemed to have a loud, passionate marriage. Very different but also stable and loving. These were what normal marriages were like.

The opposite of hers.

The breakthrough stung Grace like salt water on an open wound. Her marriage had been all wrong. Her parents had been conservative and respectful of each other, and Grace had taken that and them for granted, not really noticing their affection. But it had been there. It took these families here in San Felipe, Mexico, to remind her what a marriage was supposed to look like. The opposite of hers!

How could she not have noticed what was missing?

"Don't you think so, Grace?" Dr. Novak asked.

"What's that?" she asked, startled.

"The name, *La Hacienda de Esperanza,*" he said.

"Oh, yes. It's a beautiful name. And now that I've met you, I see it fits perfectly," Grace said.

"That's sweet," Petra said. "Would you like to see my antique plate collection?" When Grace nodded, Petra urged, "Bring your sherry with you."

"Great," Grace said, happily evading her dismal thoughts. She'd had her head in the sand the past two years.

"How about a cigar and cognac on the *pórtico?*" Poncho asked Ryan.

"May I show Grace the view from the *pórtico* first?" he answered.

"Of course!" Petra and Poncho said simultaneously.

Ryan took Grace's glass and set it down as he took her arm in his and guided her outside through double doors.

"The view's gorgeous," Grace said, pulling her arm free. She didn't want him to feel her trembling. She'd been a bigger fool than she'd thought.

"That's what I was thinking," he said, not taking his gaze from her.

She faced him. His expression, full of warmth, caused her concern. "I've never seen you in slacks or a shirt with fewer than three colors," she said, hoping to lighten the mood.

"I look out of place, do I?"

You look hot! As if he didn't know that. "It's a different side of you." *I'm the one who's out of place.*

"Are you okay? You looked a little overwhelmed in there," he said.

He'd witnessed her horrifying inner revelation. She hoped he didn't press the matter. "I'm fine. They're friendly people." Grace deflected her gaze from his handsome face. But she still inhaled his aftershave, and her reaction to his nearness upset her further. She shouldn't have come outside with him. She shouldn't have come to this house with him.

"I'm pleased we came tonight," he said.

I'm not. Her heart pounded. "Petra's lovely," she agreed. Why was he staring at her so intently? Had *he* figured out that her marriage had been a sham too? She felt her cheeks redden.

"There's something special about you, Grace." His husky voice invaded her worrisome thoughts.

Grace blinked. She glanced into his eyes and knew she *had* to intercept him from speaking his feelings.

"What's special about an ordinary widow who has yet to come to grips with reality?" she asked. "The husband I loved is gone."

He sobered immediately. He straightened and cleared his throat. "I . . . I meant you're . . . a special nurse."

"Thank you. I'll let you enjoy that cigar now."

Grace had many things to sort out, and she couldn't do it this close to a tempting, skirt-chasing doctor. A doctor who held control over the job she needed.

Chapter Nine

By the time the rooster crowed the next morning, Grace hadn't slept, but she had convinced herself not to feel any further sadness over her hoax of a marriage. And she was ready to enact a self-preservation plan.

To avoid future heartache and humiliation, she had to protect herself—from one man. Dr. Novak was too much a part of her life. The two of them truly were in each other's company twenty-four/seven. They worked together, exercised together, ate meals together, lived together, and now they had socialized together. Naturally she would seem inviting to him. He'd tricked his brain into believing she was the only game in town. Grace simply had to distance herself from Dr. Novak.

Rule number one of her plan became: don't spend time off together.

Rule number two: she had to try harder at appearing uninterested. She had to try harder at not noticing things about Dr. Novak that she admired. Forget his intelligence. Don't think about his work ethic. And especially don't think about his perfect body. Didn't those traits fit other doctors she knew? Of course they did. And she knew what kind of men they were. Ryan Novak was no different. She'd been foolish to think otherwise.

And, most important, rule number three . . .

The knock on her door caused Grace to jump. "Yes?"

"Are you ready?" Dr. Novak asked.

Wouldn't I be out there if I were ready? "Not yet." She glanced at the clock. Seven in the morning. Patients were not scheduled until nine. She promptly dressed.

Ryan paced as he waited for Grace to emerge from her bedroom.

He'd nearly made an imbecile of himself last night. Maybe in her eyes he actually had. He'd recklessly wanted to kiss Grace, and she'd stopped him cold. *Thank God.* Where had his common sense gone? Grace had made it clear: she still mourned her late husband. He sure as hell looked forward to his date with Mandy and her friends that night. Too bad he had already invited Grace along. How was he supposed to get Grace out of his system if she was always at his side?

"Good morning," she said.

He spun to see Grace in her uniform. Only Grace could make a plain white pants suit look attractive.

"After our patients this morning, we're off to La Trinidad for the afternoon," he said.

"For physicals. I'm looking forward to it."

"And we have PPD tests with us today."

"So we'll be driving back there in three days?"

"You got it."

Ryan had prepared a pharmacology pediatric conversion training lesson for Grace to review between patients. She caught on rapidly but didn't have much confidence in herself yet. He hadn't seen her self-doubt before.

Father Sanchez stopped by to bless the two of them for their life-saving actions and to check on Señor Garza's condition.

"His Mexicali doctor tells me he will be released in a week," Ryan informed him.

"Muy bien," Father Sanchez said. *Very good.*

Ryan's cell phone rang. He snatched it from his pocket. "It's Chad. Excuse me, Father. Sometimes I curse when I talk to my brother." As Ryan stepped outside, he wondered if Grace remembered the way they had looked at each other before she spotted Señor Garza in trouble. She dispassionately tucked her lesson plans into the desk drawer and smiled at Father Sanchez. Obviously not.

"Are you adjusting to life in San Felipe?" Father Sanchez asked her. His gentle tone and understanding eyes asked what his words did not.

"I'm trying, Father. But . . ." Grace wrung her hands. She didn't want to dump her problems on this kind man. "I'm not doing as well as I'd like."

He took her hands in his. "Healing takes time, my dear. It is natural to feel out of sorts. You must miss your late husband very much."

The observation struck Grace. "I loved him so." But she did not miss him anymore. She glanced away from Father Sanchez's wise gaze. Would he comfort her if he knew she had been preoccupied with Dr. Novak? No. Grace felt like a fraud again. However, she was too embarrassed to confide to anyone that her husband hadn't returned her love. And she was determined to stop loving him.

"We were only married two years." *How long would we have stayed married if he hadn't died?*

"Two years is enough time to feel immense loss."

She did feel immense loss, but not in the way the Father meant. She could not describe it. It was something lodged deep inside her that she could not yet reach. On the one hand she wanted to yank it out and be free of it. On the other she wanted to keep it buried where it couldn't hurt her.

Father Sanchez embraced her, patting her back. "Please visit me anytime you need to talk."

"Thank you, Father." She felt better.

Ryan emerged and bragged about his brother's latest accomplishments. Father Sanchez chatted for a while, then departed.

After lunch they piled their supplies and equipment into the Jeep and drove off. The families of La Trinidad welcomed them, and the hours passed swiftly.

"Performing physicals on these kids is so much fun," Grace said. "They're a hoot."

"This is the first physical exam since birth for many of them. And I suspect our state-of-the-art instruments seem odd." He tapped the tuning fork against a chair. The sound reverberated between them, and she smiled at his self-deprecating joke about the equipment.

"I'll admit you're the only doctor I've ever seen put a tongue depressor into anyone's mouth and actually utter the words, 'Say *ah*.' "

"You're kidding! How do they check tonsils in California?"

"Hmm. I'll let you know when I find out," she said.

"The kids here in Mexico seem to enjoy saying *ah*," he said.

Grace laughed. They *had* gotten melodramatic, sticking their tongues out for him.

She couldn't remember ever enjoying nursing as much as she had since coming to San Felipe. "Working here is so rewarding," she said, instantly wishing she hadn't sounded so wistful.

"I don't think I could go back," he admitted.

No, Grace couldn't imagine him working under the constraints of a hospital's hierarchy. "I know what you mean." She had no choice, but she didn't want to think about returning to that life.

He gazed at her. "This place has a way of growing on you."

Grace nodded, not trusting her voice. *So do you.* But Grace couldn't allow him to grow on her. She knew better.

"It's the children. They're so alive and so appreciative," he said.

"Yes, the children are great. I'm happy I'm here helping."

He met her gaze. "Grace, about last night . . ."

"I enjoyed meeting Petra. It was a wonderful evening," she said, quickly turning away. "I'll see if there are any more patients waiting." She left Ryan staring after her. *Running away again?* Since when had she become such a coward?

When they arrived back at La Clínica Pediátrica, Mandy and her friends rose from sitting on the porch.

"We thought you forgot about us," Mandy said. She offered her hand to Grace. "Hi. I'm Mandy."

"Yes, I remember. I'm Grace." She felt her cheeks blush. "I hope we can forget about . . . you know."

"My first bar fight will always be fondly remembered." Mandy introduced Grace to her friends, two guys and two girls. "The five of us often vacation together. But this one has been the most fun."

Grace caught the smile between Mandy and Dr. Novak. He seemed instantly elated to see Mandy. Grace felt jealous. She knew they had spent time enjoying each other's company not too many nights ago. She wondered if that was the most fun Dr. Novak had had since coming to this tiny village.

"Give us a few minutes to freshen up," Dr. Novak said.

"I believe you promised to give me a tour of your clinic," Mandy said.

"Oh, that's right," Ryan said.

"Besides, I'm sure Grace needs more than 'a few minutes' to freshen up," Mandy said with a glimmer in her eyes.

Grace considered taking another swing at the woman. But she did need more time than the doctor to get dressed. And, more important, she wanted the pair to have time alone . . . time to rekindle whatever flame they had ignited. Didn't she?

"I appreciate that, Mandy," Grace said as cheerfully as she could.

"We'll wait in the cantina," one of Mandy's friends said. The group laughed on their way to the cantina.

Grace opened the Jeep's back door.

"I'll get the supplies," Ryan said.

"I can help," Grace said.

"Don't need help."

"Then let me unlock the clinic."

Ryan dug into his pocket and handed her his keys.

Their hands briefly touched. Grace felt a quiver shoot through her body. His touch transmitted both warmth and strength. In that moment she knew it would be heaven to really be held in his arms. And she knew she needed to steer clear of that embrace. *Lucky Mandy.*

She went ahead inside, not wanting to hear Mandy's flirtatious chatter. She and Ryan followed her in, and Grace heard them talking. Mandy sounded impressed by everything the doctor said. Rolling her eyes, Grace hurried to tally the supplies used and to restock.

Mandy let her attraction for Dr. Novak show, completely unconcerned that Grace occupied the same space. Just like . . . An old, painful memory was dredged up, and Grace quickly dismissed it.

Mandy laughed. Then he laughed. They made a nice, phony couple. Deep down she felt Mandy wasn't right for him. But her opinion didn't matter. Grace shouldn't care about Mandy's and Dr. Novak's business.

The group "date" tonight would be the bucket of ice she required to convince herself that Ryan Novak was a flirting Casanova. The kind that could only break a woman's heart.

She'd seen another side of him yesterday, a wonderful, loyal, and loving side, but he had also told her previously that he didn't want a woman encumbering his life. That proved his interests lay in a short fling.

"You're not looking forward to this evening, are you?" he asked as he locked the medications in the cabinet.

"Yes, I am," she lied. "I'm really excited about . . . what are we doing?"

He laughed. She glanced up from the supplies. "You're not very good at lying," he said.

"Where I come from, that's considered a compliment." She glimpsed around. "What happened to Mandy?"

"I kept the tour short and asked her to wait for us at the cantina."

"Oh. I guess I should get ready." Grace turned and marched into her room for a change of clothes before taking a quick shower.

Ryan knocked on her door. "We're having a clambake on the beach."

"Isn't that a bit of a cliché?"

"They're tourists," he said.

When they arrived at the cantina, Mandy covered her face with her hands as her friends laughed hysterically at something Carmen had told them. Gabriel and Benita nodded their heads, confirming Carmen's story.

Benita looked as if her flu had passed, Grace thought, as the young woman smiled at them.

"Graciela, come in. You need to hear this *también*," *too,* Carmen said.

"Oh, no." Ryan groaned.

"Sorry," Gabriel said. "Can I get you something?"

"No. We're not staying," Ryan replied.

"Dr. Novak, you held out on us!" Mandy said.

"For good reason," he said. "You ready to hit the beach?"

"Not yet," Mandy and her friends shouted.

"What did I miss?" Grace asked Carmen, disregarding Dr. Novak's frown.

"I was telling them about the crazy woman who came here to steal away our doctor's heart."

Grace glanced at Mandy, then returned her attention to Carmen and Benita. "What crazy woman?"

"Never mind," Dr. Novak said, clearly unamused. "We don't want to miss the sunset."

"Hold your horses," Carmen said, enjoying the spotlight. "Several weeks ago a woman arrived in San Felipe, pretending to be a nurse. She said the employment agency had sent her, and she had dropped by, uninvited, for an interview."

Grace gasped. The others giggled. That must have been just before she'd arrived.

"The smart doctor identified her trickery and sent her home before she could unpack. So, the lady came in here to use *el teléfono,* and her suitcase fell open. That is when we all saw the wedding gown she had brought with her!"

Mandy and her friends joined the laughter of Carmen and Gabriel. Grace saw the humor in the situation, but she also understood what Dr. Novak had been going through before she arrived. "All because of the contest?"

"*Sí,*" Carmen said.

Grace wondered if she could ever have such nerve.

"Did he tell you about his fan mail and—"

"Some other time, Carmen," Dr. Novak said, as he rose.

"And I thought I was the first," Mandy said, rising and hooking her arm in Ryan's. "Though I confess, we came mainly for the beach. Finding you was a pleasant surprise." She kept a tight grip on him as they headed for the beach.

Mandy's friends included Grace in their conversation as they strolled toward the sea. But Grace's thoughts wandered. Could Internet contest photos really possess women to take such drastic actions?

To his credit, Dr. Novak appeared truly bothered by the behavior rather than flattered. That alone set him apart from most men she knew.

The odd thing was, Dr. Novak didn't seem to realize that these nervy women were probably exactly his type. The kind who took risks, who set their mind to something and followed through, and who possessed infallible confidence. Unlike Grace.

Two hours later Grace felt completely disconcerted. Her entire purpose in the evening was to see for herself what a jerk Ryan Novak really was. Seeing him pursuing another woman was supposed to douse any fantasies that showed any tendency to grow.

Instead, Dr. Novak paid no special attention to Mandy. He handled all the tourists like old chums. The pretty Mandy openly flirted with him, but he didn't bite. But Mandy was persistent.

"I hear music coming from the nightclub," Mandy said. "It sounds like such a romantic ballad."

"Mariachis play on the weekends," Dr. Novak said.

"You found us the perfect spot." Mandy squeezed his arm. "The music, the beach with a gorgeous sunset, and proximity to the bar. I didn't know one could get bar service on the beach."

"Only in paradise," John, Mandy's friend, said. He tapped one of the girls on the shoulder. "Let's go dance." All the friends jumped at the opportunity to party. They pranced over to the club with the outdoor dance floor.

The music had livened up. Mandy grabbed Dr. Novak's arm. "Come on."

"I need my dancing partner," he said, putting his hand out to Grace.

Dancing had always lifted her spirits. But even after one margarita, Grace didn't want to compete for a man on the dance floor. Especially for a man she didn't want. "You two go ahead." She'd watch for a minute or so, then sneak back to the clinic.

Dr. Novak surprised Grace by frowning at her. He took Mandy's hand, and they found their way onto the parquet floor. Mandy let loose, moving her hips provocatively. Dr. Novak stopped fighting her advances, and they swayed to the music.

Grace felt ridiculous. *Great way to act as if he has no effect on me.* In fact, she'd drawn more attention to herself by turning him down than by dancing.

She needn't have worried.

Mandy clasped his waist from behind and rubbed her body against him, gaining his undivided attention. She ran her other hand up and down his thigh. They looked great together, just as Grace had imagined they would.

Mandy tossed her head back and laughed. He laughed too.

Grace was pleased to see Dr. Novak and Mandy finally hit it off. This was what she needed to see. This was what would immunize her from catching the Dr. Novak fever.

Then why did she feel sick to her stomach? Grace didn't understand. What more did she need to get this man out of her psyche? Perhaps she was using the wrong strategy. Perhaps she should dance with him herself and confirm that she had no chance of catching Novak fever.

"John!" Dr. Novak called Mandy's friend.

John took over dancing with Mandy.

Ryan's gaze found Grace, and she watched him approach her. She swallowed hard as he offered his arm to her.

She hooked her arm in his. One quick dance and she'd leave. She didn't like breaking her own rules the same day she made them. *Rules meant to thwart me from making unwise choices.*

The music slowed, and Ryan pulled Grace close. His arms encircled her, and Grace thought she would melt into him. Being pressed against his strong chest made her pulse race. Every nerve ending within her sparked. His scent filled her consciousness. Grace knew she should stop dancing, stop gazing into his eyes, and cool off. Instead, she snaked her arms around his neck and danced with him.

His gaze smoldered. Her emotions spun wildly. She felt both apprehension and excitement. He lowered his head, and his breath fanned her face. If she leaned forward a fraction, their lips would meet.

Everything about Ryan Novak seemed honorable. But she'd been wrong before. Dreadfully wrong. She would not make the same mistake.

Grace stepped back. She caught his brief expression of hurt, making her feel awful. What could she say? *I'm just making sure I can resist you?*

"How about a walk?" he said.

"What about Mandy?"

"She's with her friends." He clasped her hand, leading her onto the sandy beach.

Grace took a moment to deal with her own dejection. As she predicted, it had felt heavenly in his arms. She took long strides toward the sea, as if that would somehow help.

The tide rushed in noisily and quietly withdrew. Just like her emotions around Dr. Novak. She'd excitedly rushed into his arms, only to quietly realize she didn't belong there. She pulled her hand free.

"Now that you've seen both, do you prefer the sunrise or the sunset?"

Her gaze lingered on the orange ball descending into the horizon. The glow was reflected in the sea. "Both are magnificent." Or maybe it was just the man beside her that made daily events seem miraculous. *The same man who had the power to send her packing if she displeased him.* "I haven't decided yet."

"You take a while to make a decision, don't you?"

"Not for everything," she said defensively.

"Just make a choice."

"Can't I enjoy both?"

"Sure. But I prefer to make a choice and fully commit to that one," he said.

Easy for a man to say, she thought. *Not so easy for him to do.* "You use the word *commit* rather freely. What happens if you see the other one again. Do you change your mind?"

"I trust my judgment. And I honor my commitments."

Maybe that was her problem; she no longer trusted her judgment. "I know people who intend to honor a commitment. But when it no longer suits their needs, they make new choices."

"I'm not one of those people." His unfaltering gaze searched hers. "We're talking about two different things here, aren't we?" he asked.

Her heart pounded. Grace didn't want to talk about being deceived by a husband who had made her believe he loved her. Made her believe he was committed to their marriage. The worst part was, Grace couldn't even ask what she'd done wrong. Before she could confront him, or deter him from leaving, or at least strangle him, he had died in the accident that left her a widow.

"No." She bit her lip.

He came to a stop, and Grace halted automatically. He eyed her a moment. "Are you jealous of Mandy?"

Grace blinked. "I'm not jealous, you moron."

"You could have fooled me."

"Why, because I'm not falling into your arms? Have you forgotten I'm only recently a widow?"

Ryan observed the fiery look in her eyes. He'd pushed her hot button. "Yes. I forgot. Because back there you . . ."

"You were the one dragging me on your date. I think you're afraid of Mandy."

Now Grace had jerked *his* chain. He didn't like it. "Wanting to avoid complications doesn't make me afraid."

"Then ditto for me! Avoiding complications doesn't make me jealous."

She'd gotten him. Ryan knew what he was avoiding—and covering up from his past—which he had no intention of discussing. But he hadn't figured out what Grace had to cover up. "That's a nice bit of dancing around the issue, but I liked it better when we danced for real. Don't you agree?"

"What?"

He enjoyed taking the wind out of her sails.

"Grace . . ." He paused, brushing away strands of hair from her face. He noted the softness of her hair; it was just as he had anticipated. He wished she'd wear it loose from her ponytail.

"What?" Her breaths quickened as she took a half step back.

He knew he should give her more time. He knew he should give her more space. Lots of it. But she had his head spinning. "The look on your face . . . I could see jealousy."

"You're imagining things!" Her eyes flashed.

"You want something, then you don't."

"I'm not one of your Internet fans. I'm not the type to swoon at your feet."

"I'm not asking you to."

He didn't know what he was asking. He'd already had to call upon all his willpower not to kiss her while they danced. Though she'd given him signals that suggested otherwise, Grace had already told him no. He was obligated to ignore his instincts.

"You have nothing to be jealous about." He knew he sounded like a conceited idiot. But he could not complete his thought aloud: *Mandy could never measure up to you*.

"Well, hallelujah. Such a humble statement from a self-absorbed doctor."

"That came out wrong."

"I don't see how it could possibly come out right." Grace laughed. "I'm sure Mandy is wondering where her 'hot' doctor has wandered off to."

He looked hard at her. "I mustn't keep her waiting." He turned and walked away.

Chapter Ten

Dr. Novak had rewarded Grace with a hard stare before he turned and strode away from her. The sun had long since set, and in the darkness a cool breeze gave Grace a chill. She'd encouraged the vain Dr. Novak to rejoin Mandy, and he'd eagerly taken her suggestion. It seemed he couldn't get away from Grace fast enough.

Grace headed for La Clínica Pediátrica. The uphill path seemed to reflect her life ahead. She didn't have the key, but she could wait on the porch. She needed to clear her thoughts.

Grace had never felt more heated around a man than she did with Ryan Novak. His passionate gaze had told her what he wanted to do. And she had relished every minute of it.

Except Grace didn't want passion from Ryan Novak. She'd been down this road before. She could not survive another failure at love. Yet . . . she couldn't stop the longing.

Longing? Is that what he'd seen in her expression that

he'd mistaken for jealousy? Grace groaned. Neither emotion fit. Neither was suitable for a nurse and her employer doctor.

Maybe she needed to change careers. That was the only way to ensure she wasn't around doctors flirting with nurses, reliving every day what her husband had been doing behind her back. And around the relentless gossiping that had hurt almost as much.

"I'll make you a copy of the clinic key tomorrow," Ryan said, startling Grace.

How long had he been standing there, watching her?

"Thank you."

He set down the picnic items and unlocked the door. "Don't worry. I'm through with putting my foot in my mouth for the night."

She swallowed. Not daring to speak or smile, Grace went to her room. She hated being vulnerable in front of any doctor. She'd perfected her all-business persona for a reason. To keep skirt-chasing doctors away. Once they saw your soft side, they took that as a sign of gullibility, of vulnerability.

Grace had nearly succumbed to Dr. Novak's charisma. And somehow she'd have to resist it the remaining forty-plus weeks of her contract.

As she slipped under her covers, she heard him in his room. He was more active than usual, like a caged animal during a full moon. Grace longed to call his name, but that went against her logic and purpose for coming to San Felipe.

She remembered his gaze on her face, his strong arms around her. She tossed and turned, trying to remove his image from her mind. But she could not, which was insane. She hardly knew the man. He certainly didn't know her beyond their work lives. Any attraction between them was entirely physical.

Actually, though, she didn't have anything more to offer than her physical self. Her passion had died. She had no heart left. Could she cope with a relationship based on physical attraction? *No.* That went against everything she believed in.

She sat up. But if she wasn't offering him her heart, she couldn't get hurt. *No.* She would be a fool to try. Or was she a fool for not trying?

Dr. Novak would disapprove of her indecision.

As if he could hear her thoughts, he bumped against something and cursed.

Ryan awoke tired and grumpy. He'd had a heck of a night. He resisted the temptation to barge into Grace's room and ask her what game she was playing. He knew he couldn't handle her looking at him with those big brown eyes and seeing her part her soft, pouty lips.

Damn. He flung off the bedspread and rose. He tugged on his pants, leaving his clothes from yesterday on the floor. He stumbled on the bedspread and kicked it.

He didn't care how much noise he made. He hoped she'd had a restless night too. The heck with shaving. He'd take a quick shower and get started.

The shower stall had water drops on the walls. The soap felt moist. Grace had been there already. He brought the bar of soap up to his nose and inhaled, hoping to get a whiff of Grace's scent. The bar slipped from his grasp, and he cursed again.

How the heck did he end up with Grace in his arms

anyway? Hadn't he planned to let Mandy take his mind off his lovely nurse? A nurse who didn't want anything to do with him. The same nurse who'd told him she still loved her husband.

He'd bet his best poker hand that Grace had progressed beyond mourning her late husband. Now that he thought about it, she never wore a wedding ring. Then why had she said *stop?*

Once more he sensed that she was hiding something huge. Ryan had his patients to think about. What if what she concealed had to do with her nursing abilities? No. That wasn't the issue. Some other skeleton rattled in Grace's closet.

He dried himself off and redressed in his wrinkled khaki pants and shirt. He had no choice but to confront her. She was his employee, and he had a right to know.

His damp flip-flops squeaked on the hardwood floor as he approached her. Not exactly the formidable entrance he wanted.

She wore her crisp uniform and looked well rested.

"We need to talk," he said irritably.

She blinked at him.

"What are you hiding from me?"

"Nothing that concerns you or my ability to work in this clinic."

He liked the way she bluntly stated her case.

"I'll be the one to determine that," he said.

Her chin rose. "If the question wasn't on my application, then there's no need for you to be concerned about the answer."

Darn her. He was losing ground. "Mistrust affects our working relationship. How can I give you a key to my clinic, let alone let you assist my patients, if I can't trust you?"

"Can't trust *me?*" Grace looked completely shaken, making him rethink his demand to know about her past.

Her gaze went downward.

No! He didn't want her to lose her spunk or her pride.

"Can you give me your word that whatever your secret is, it won't affect my patients?"

"Yes. I give you my word."

"What happened last night?" he asked.

"Excuse me?"

"On the porch last night, you looked like you needed a friend, and yet you'd turned away."

"I'm fine now," she said.

He doubted that. But the realization hit him that Grace did not trust *him*.

"Good, let's get to work, then," he said, determined to stop thinking about how right she had felt in his arms.

She handed him a chart. "Jaime's first on the schedule. We're checking his wounds for signs of infection, making sure those sutures are dissolving, and removing the Steri Strips."

"Carmen will be in this morning to pick up an allergy kit for Chiquita," he said, noting that Grace smelled as fresh as the sea she loved. He wanted to brush back the wisps of hair that had fallen from her clip.

"I'll have it ready for her."

A rattling noise caught his attention.

Glass hitting glass or metal.

"Is that what I think it is?" Grace asked.

The rattling grew in intensity. The vibrations caused furniture to scrape across the floor. The roof creaked.

"Under the table, quick." Ryan pulled Grace under the only sturdy table in the waiting room. They heard glass and books and equipment crash to the floor in the other rooms. A window shattered and smashed on the table above them. "Close your eyes!"

"Terremoto!" someone outside screamed.

Grace knew that word. *Earthquake!*

Ryan held on to the table to prevent it from jostling away from them. More shouts and screams came from outside.

"We have to help them," Grace said.

"Not yet."

Ugly crashing sounds from outside had Ryan saying prayers.

The church bell rang wildly, then went silent for a long, painful moment until they heard a loud boom.

"The school! The young ones are in the school!" Grace tried to run out.

Ryan grabbed her arm. "Not yet. We can't help others if we're victims ourselves." He held her tightly. Another window exploded, sending a shower of glass inward. Ryan protected Grace with his body.

The roof strained, and a floorboard burst upward. The entire building shook. "My God! Stay close, Grace."

Livestock squealed and squawked. The clinic swayed as if it were a boat out at sea. A rough sea. Finally the movement stopped, but the villagers' frantic shouts continued.

"Are you okay?" He pulled Grace out.

She nodded. "The people, the kids . . ."

"Listen. We need to put the first-aid cases onto the luggage carts so we have mobility." He clicked a number into his cell phone as he followed her to the storage closet.

"We stay together, and remember, more injuries come from aftershocks."

Grace moved fast.

"Mexicali ER? Dr. Novak here of La Clínica Pediátrica. San Felipe has just experienced a quake, a big one. We need help. We'll need supplies."

Ryan listened as he watched Grace load extra supplies into the cases. Her hands trembled. He covered one with his, and she glanced at him. "I may not be able to call again. Please notify Mexico City for EMR activation. Thank you." He disconnected the call.

"We'll be okay," he said. "Mexico has an Emergency Medical Response plan for situations like this. But we're on our own until help arrives."

"I can handle trauma. I worked in the ER, remember?"

For mere weeks, probably, he thought. A brief rotation. Grace already sounded stressed. He'd have to keep an eye on her. He didn't need her breaking down from mental strain.

"Aftershocks are our worst enemy. Keep away from dangerous structures so we can help everyone, okay?"

"Yes, Doctor."

"Put extra masking tape and markers in the side pockets while I get more medications."

He ran into a damaged exam room. His storage table and all the tools on top of it had fallen over. Thank God he had bolted down the medicine cabinet. He unlocked it and removed vials of morphine, codeine, Vicodin, and penicillin. He took tablets of Tylenol, ibuprofen, and Percodan.

"Dr. Novak, hurry," Grace called.

He locked the cabinet and ran to his room. "I can't go

out there in flip-flops. I need my Rockports." He changed shoes, grabbed leather work gloves, and quickly joined her at the door.

He wasn't prepared for the sight outside.

Grace rolled her cart down the porch steps. He followed, taking in the destruction all around them.

Houses were flattened. Only adobe homes and structures in the village square remained standing. Most were severely damaged—roofs caved in, walls collapsed or curved at perilous angles. Cries for help came from all around them. So many were injured. He didn't know where to begin.

"The school, Doctor." Grace handed him a whistle on a cord. He kept it in a pocket of the emergency case. Instantly he remembered what to do.

He blew the whistle. The nearby villagers ran to him, including Gabriel and Carmen. "We need to account for everyone," he told them. "The injured who can walk should gather outside the clinic. The injured who are trapped must be safely freed. Watch for weakened structures. I need two strong men to join us at the school." Dr. Novak repeated the commands in Spanish.

"I will go," Gabriel said.

"No. I need you to organize the others," Dr. Novak said, handing him the whistle.

Gabriel looked at it as if Ryan had handed him a bag of gold, and he blew the whistle hard.

Everyone moved into action.

"Chiquita is at the school!" Carmen said.

"Please help out here. We will find her—I promise," Ryan said. He meant it.

"Thank you."

John, Mandy, and her friends ran toward him. "How can we help?" John asked.

"Gabriel's in charge of rescue efforts. He'll need all able hands."

"I'm bleeding," Mandy said, clearly frightened. Her arm had a superficial abrasion.

"It's just a scratch. We're needed at the school," he said.

"I need you to examine me." Mandy's pitch increased.

Grace impatiently took off.

"When we return. You'll be fine for now." He didn't have time to deal with her hysteria.

He hurried alongside Grace and the two villagers. When the school came into view, Ryan's hopes plummeted.

Chapter Eleven

At least the church bell hadn't fallen on top of the school, he thought. But most of the tile roof had collapsed.

"It was solidly built with a strong foundation," he said of the structure.

Grace pointed at a crack in the ground bordering the damaged school building. "That crack wasn't there before."

"Is that a fault line?" Ryan wondered aloud.

As they neared, Ryan heard children's cries for help. Debris buried the front door. "Look for a safe way to enter."

The team split in either direction. As Ryan and Grace hurried to the left, the cries became louder. The caved-in roof had crushed the windows and crumpled the wall down to four feet high.

"Tell me they were taught to take cover under their desks," Grace said.

Ryan didn't respond. These were the kindergartners. His heart battered against his chest.

"Señora Lopez!" Ryan shouted. "Kids, we're going to help you!"

They reached the back door. The ground had lifted in a mound of solid rock, preventing the door from opening.

"Doctor! We can enter through windows," one of the men said in Spanish. "Over here."

Ryan and Grace sprinted to the right of the structure. This side of the building had withstood the quake better. At least the roof hadn't buckled completely and pancaked the wall.

Ryan reached inside a broken window and unlocked it. Grace did the same for the second window. He slid them open to avoid the sharp, jagged pieces of glass. He yanked the leather gloves from his back pocket and swiped away bits of glass from both sills. Grace hoisted herself into the classroom.

Inside, five- and six-year-olds cried but could not be seen. Ryan spoke soothingly to them as he climbed in.

"Wait here. You'll help the kids out the windows," he said to the men outside. "We must account for each child."

A slight tremble of the earth and a tile bursting from the floor prodded him not to waste time. Grace crouched to see under the desks, and he did the same. The sight constricted his throat.

The children cowered in fear under their desks. The ones near the left wall had debris upon them.

"Señora Lopez is hurt," young Chiquita said.

Grace glanced in the direction Chiquita pointed.

Before Ryan could say anything, Grace slithered under fallen beams and debris to find the teacher. "Wait!" he called.

But she slipped out of sight.

His pulse beat rapidly. "Grace, get back here."

"Let me see if I can reach her."

Damn. He'd have to reprimand her for taking such a risk. "Is everyone else okay?" he asked Chiquita.

"I don't know."

On hands and knees Ryan reached the little girl.

"Kids. One by one, let's go." Chiquita and the closest row of kids easily slipped free. One villager had climbed in to help the children over the sill. Ryan handed each child to the other man and the distraught parents who had gathered outside.

Ryan glanced at a creaking beam overhead. One end of the beam at the back of the room touched the floor; the other end, at the front of the room, barely held on to the ceiling. "Grace?" he called out.

"She's unconscious, and she's trapped!" Grace called back to him.

"Come back out of there. I'll get her."

"You can't fit through the opening. Her vitals are weak."

"Come out now. An aftershock could . . ."

"Wait," Grace said. He heard a small muffled voice and something scraping across the floor. Then Grace said to someone under the rubble, "Can you reach me?"

More scraping. The beam creaked menacingly above. Ryan felt a drop of perspiration trickle down his back. If anything happened to Grace . . .

He had to think of the children first.

The second row of kids moved more slowly; they had more rubble to get through, and one had injuries.

"Doctor, my arm," one boy said. "It hurts bad."

"I'll help you outside," Ryan said. "Careful lifting him," he said to the men, as they continued to evacuate the children.

"Talk to me, Grace."

"Mrs. Lopez is definitely trapped, and there're more kids under here."

"Don't move anything! I'll help you in a minute."

He crawled deeper into the pulverized classroom.

The row of desks along the left windows had the wreckage of the roof on top of them.

"Is everyone okay?" he asked.

Four or five voices replied, *"Sí, Doctor."*

"Come carefully toward my voice. Don't touch anything." He hated not having visual contact with the children or with Grace. He still heard her soft voice, guiding a child to crawl to her.

He felt a rumble beneath his hands. The floor shook. He knew the loosened beam was directly above himself and Grace. "Grace, an aftershock!" He curled himself under a desk. "Kids, stay under the desks. Cover your heads!"

The schoolhouse shook violently. He hoped the men had moved the freed kids to safety. They wouldn't hear his voice over the sound of the crashing tiles and the fracturing floor. Outside, the church and other structures rattled in protest.

The wood beam fell.

It smashed onto the teacher's oak desk and the second

row of pupils' desks, deluging them with more tiles and debris. He couldn't see through the dust.

Kids coughed. They were alive!

"Grace!"

More coughing.

Parents' screams reached him from outside.

"Grace!" he gasped.

The aftershock ended, and thick clouds of dust swarmed everywhere.

Children's cries . . . the villagers' voices . . . the sound of debris being hurriedly cleared . . . With his throat clogged, Ryan couldn't call out anymore.

"I think we're okay," Grace called. Then she coughed.

Hearing her voice, he could breathe again.

"Doctor!" the men outside shouted. "Is everyone okay in there?"

Ryan waved dust away. "Kids, are you all right?"

Several voices responded.

"We're okay!" he shouted, glancing around him. Somehow the intact desks were holding the beam about three feet above the floor. He worried that the next aftershock would dislodge it.

"Can I still send the kids out the same way?" he called out.

He heard movement behind him, then saw a ray of sunlight as villagers moved the new rubble aside. "Yes."

He cleared a passage to the first child, anxious to get them all out of there. He knew the villagers worked behind him to fortify what was left of the perilously low roof and prevent the beam from closing off their path.

Two kids smiled at him. One had a gash on his forearm.

"When you get outside, put your hand over this and press hard." Ryan took the child's good hand and placed it over the gash. "I'll help you when all your friends are safe."

The child nodded.

"One at a time. How many behind you?"

"Six in my line, but Lupe won't answer," the boy said.

"Where was she before the quake?"

The child thought a moment. "At the chalkboard."

Ryan directed them to the small opening ahead. He realized that the teacher, Señora Lopez, must have come out from under her desk to protect Lupe.

"Grace, who do you have?"

"Lupe. I'm bringing her out."

"No. I'll come to you." He pulled out the next frightened child, who suffered from lacerations and a twisted ankle.

The next child had fragments of glass sprinkled on his bloody shirt and complained of something hitting him. Ryan expected to find cuts and bruises but no broken bones under that shirt. The final child pulled through unscathed.

Ryan confirmed there were no others left behind as Lupe and Grace appeared.

"Broken radius, I think," Grace said.

"I told you not to move." He saw that Grace had used the classroom flag to pull Lupe out. The overwhelming relief he felt at seeing Grace unharmed astounded him. He wanted to gather her into his arms and scold her for putting herself in danger.

Instead he scowled at her as he took the child.

"I need this back," she said, extracting the flag from his grasp.

"You're not going back in there."

"You won't fit, and we can't leave her."

He touched Grace's arm. "Can you move her safely? There's a crew outside working their way through this mess."

"They could make the wrong move and topple the whole thing."

He knew that. And he sure as hell didn't want Grace in there if that happened.

"I'll drag Señora Lopez as far as I can with the flag. You'll need to pull her from your end."

"Wait for me." Ryan turned, pulling Lupe like a drowning victim toward the men outside. As he slithered toward the window, one of the villagers reached in and took Lupe.

"Shall we come inside to help you?" the villager asked.

"No. It's too unstable," Ryan said, withdrawing to rescue Grace.

The building trembled ever so slightly. If he weren't sprawled on the floor, he might not have felt it.

Ryan knew Grace was in danger. "Be careful. As your employer, I'm responsible for you, you know."

"I'm responsible for myself," she said.

He wanted to say more. Instead, he followed her voice as far as he could and waited.

Dust trickled down, and the desks and the floor creaked. It occurred to him that they were in danger of the damaged floor collapsing beneath them.

He heard Grace's movements. He groped the ground

as far ahead as he could reach. Finally he touched Señora Lopez's hair. "Keep her as straight as you can," he urged Grace.

He bunched the fabric of the flag in one fist and pulled as Grace pushed. Dust rained upon them. He held his breath. At last he got a grip on the flag with both hands. Together they hauled Señora Lopez to safety. The teacher regained consciousness and moaned.

Once outside, they were greeted with hugs from appreciative parents of the schoolchildren.

"Muchas personas esperen en la clínica." A villager announced that several injured people awaited the doctor's return at the clinic.

As Ryan examined Señora Lopez, he glanced up at Grace. Dirt smudged her hair and face. Her white uniform was filthy and wilted. She, however, stood firm and triumphant. Surely no woman had ever looked more beautiful.

"Good job, Grace. But our work has just begun."

Parents of the victims wanted their crying children treated immediately. Others waited patiently.

Grace stooped and opened one of the black cases. "Tell me what you need, Doctor."

He wished he could tell her the truth: *You, Grace. You are what I need.*

Grace shoved some books that had fallen from shelves in the school under Señora Lopez's ankles, elevating her feet. As she dabbed a bleeding wound on the teacher's head, Dr. Novak took her vitals.

He checked her pupils. "They're even and responsive."

"The children . . . Are they okay?" Señora Lopez asked weakly.

"Everyone is fine. Do you remember what happened?"

"Arithmetic lesson." She glanced around her. "Earth-quake."

Dr. Novak performed a neurological assessment on her, asking her to lift both arms and squeeze both his hands with both of hers. He asked her to close her eyes and tell her what parts of her he touched.

"My feet," she said. "My knee. My elbow."

He asked her to flex her feet, and she did, though she grimaced. He palpated her abdomen, and when she squirmed, he lifted her blouse halfway, revealing a large bruise on her left lower quadrant.

"Did anything hit your head?"

"The bookcase." She shivered. "A pupil was at the chalkboard . . . and the bookcase tipped over. I tried to hold it up, but it fell on me."

Grace covered the teacher with a sweater someone handed her.

"You did a brave thing, ma'am," Dr. Novak said. "Do you remember who the child was?" He examined the head wound that hadn't stopped bleeding.

Señora Lopez tried sitting up but rubbed her thorax and made a face. *"Una niña."* A little girl. Her gaze scanned the villagers and some of her students. Her eyes widened. "Lupe."

"Very good."

A man broke through the small crowd. "Isabel!" He ran to the teacher's side and gently lifted her hand.

"Señor Lopez, we need to carry your wife to *la clínica,* where we can treat her wounds and observe her. When the air ambulance arrives, I want her to go."

"Where? What's wrong?"

"She needs X-rays. I'm certain she has broken ribs, we're treating her for shock, and since she became unconscious after a blow to the head, I'm recommending a CT scan."

"What is that?"

"A test to see if she has any skull fractures or brain damage. I don't know for sure what hospital they're evacuating to, but my guess is Mexicali."

"May I go with her?"

"Possibly."

After asking Señor Lopez about his wife's medications and allergies, Dr. Novak injected two milligrams of morphine for pain. Grace wrote the medicine, the dose, and time on a strip of masking tape and pressed it onto Isabel Lopez's chest.

"Gracias, Doctor."

"Start an IV of normal saline TKO," he said. Grace did as he requested.

The villagers used the flag as a stretcher to carry Señora Lopez. Her husband held the IV bag above her. She clutched her lower left thorax, making Grace believe she had suffered broken ribs. She wished Señora Lopez had something to hold, like a pillow, to ease her pain.

Together they stabilized Lupe and three other children. All four of them would require further care.

At the clinic, an assortment of people waited, both tourists and villagers. Dr. Novak and Grace split up to perform the triage assessment. Two patients were placed in urgent status, which Dr. Novak tended immediately. Grace continued the triage. Five were high status; the remaining twelve were low status. Thankfully none were judged do-not-treat status, which meant that treatment would not likely save them.

Grace had the patients line up so Dr. Novak could instantly see how many he had of each and who was next. The patients accepted her judgments and waited without complaint. As time allowed, Grace assisted Dr. Novak, treating those in the high status category.

Family members helped keep an eye on the seriously wounded. Carmen had returned after taking Chiquita home. Poncho and his wife, Petra, had come into town to help. While Poncho used his truck to remove debris and search for the injured, Petra assisted Grace.

As new victims arrived, Grace triaged them and settled them in with their group. Dr. Novak and Grace kept moving, each always with a patient. She worried about him. The strain must be getting to him.

Most casualties were sent home with an envelope of ibuprofen and bandages on their cleansed wounds, except for three victims who were in need of sutures. Dr. Novak pulled Grace aside.

"Injured keep arriving. I need you to suture these victims," he said.

"Me?" Adrenaline pumped through Grace. "But . . ."

"Have you ever . . ."

"No. I'm not certified."

He called Petra over. "We'll be back in a few minutes. Keep watch for us."

"I will, Doctor," Petra said.

Dr. Novak guided Grace toward the clinic. "Coming from the ER, surely you know how?"

"I've only assisted."

"Suturing is an item on your checklist."

Grace had been excited when she read that item. But she never suspected she'd do it without proper training.

"You'll stay and guide me through it?"

"Only for the first patient."

"I can't practice on a real person!" What if she made a mistake? What if she hurt the victim?

"Grace, there's no one else. I need you to do this."

Dr. Novak didn't hire a jellyfish. Toughen up, she scolded herself. With shaky legs she followed him into the surgical exam room.

"Don't look so worried. I wouldn't ask if I wasn't completely confident in you." He sat on his stool.

She scanned his face. He did seem quite optimistic.

"If you can't do it, they'll wait forever in Mexicali, which will give them low priority," he said.

Grace wrung her hands. She knew these victims would suffer needlessly, waiting to be transported and then waiting for treatment once they arrived in Mexicali.

"How will you explain to the first patient that I don't know what I'm doing?"

"Your patient is very understanding." Dr. Novak rolled up his right shirtsleeve, revealing a gauze dressing he had clumsily applied to himself.

Grace had seen blood on his shirt but assumed it came from the quake victims.

"Dr. Novak, you're injured!"

Chapter Twelve

She hurried to get saline solution and gauze to clean his wound. "When did this happen?"

"In the school."

"Why didn't you say anything?" She removed the bloodstained dressing.

"We were busy."

"Doctors!" she huffed. She cleaned and inspected the four-inch slash on the top of his forearm.

He smiled at her.

"I bet you weren't going to say anything at all. You're only speaking up now so I can practice on you."

"You know me too well," he said.

Wearing sterile gloves, Grace gathered the items she had always prepared for doctors on the tray. He watched her without comment. When the tray had the clamps, sutures, Steri Strips, cotton balls, and Betadine splayed out, she turned to him. "EMLA Cream, right?"

"I don't keep that locked. It's in the drawer."

"You'll need penicillin."

"Yes." He handed her the cabinet keys.

Grace drew the penicillin into the syringe and administered the antibiotic. "I may as well give you the tetanus now too." She discarded the used syringe and needle.

"I'm up to date on my immunizations," he said.

"Unless you can provide proof, you're getting a shot." Grace pulled out the tetanus vaccine and withdrew .5 cc into the syringe. She tapped it, releasing the air bubble.

"I've created a monster," he mumbled.

"I heard that." She handed him the syringe and unbuttoned his shirt.

Grace forced herself to keep her hands steady. As she pulled the shirt down his left shoulder, she spurned her quickened pulse. She lifted the cap off the syringe and squeezed his firm, muscled arm. "Here it goes." She efficiently stuck him.

He fixed his shirt. "I'm ready," he said.

"In the States . . ."

"We're in Mexico. It's okay."

As she changed into fresh sterile gloves, Grace didn't bat an eyelash. Forgetting her anxiety, she concentrated on mending Dr. Novak. First she cleaned, then numbed with the topical cream, and then she sutured.

Grace had learned more than she realized from watching ER physicians and nurse practitioners and Dr. Novak himself. And his trust in her abilities gave her self-confidence a big boost.

"All done." Now that she had finished, Grace no longer had a reason to touch him. She glanced up to find he'd already been gazing at her. His expression was unlike any he'd shown before. She'd seen many things in

Ryan Novak's eyes: concern, annoyance, joy. But now they conveyed pride. In her.

Grace cleared her throat. "I suppose it's pointless to tell you to rest that arm."

He shrugged, rising.

"Hold it." Knowing that the doctor would stay active for hours, she applied a couple of Steri Strips to prevent the wound from reopening.

He stretched and examined her suturing. "You did as good a job as any specialist I know." He placed his hands on her shoulders. "You're one heck of a nurse."

His words rejuvenated her. "Thanks." She grabbed two caplets of ibuprofen and filled a paper cup with water. "Drink."

"No. We may run out." He refused the ibuprofen.

"You're my patient. If you become febrile, my confidence will be ruined." She covered the wound with a loose dressing.

He chuckled. "I'll be fine."

The sound of helicopters filled Grace with elation. The casualties would be airlifted, and supplies would be delivered.

"Ah, our medicine has arrived." He took the caplets and swallowed them with the water.

"Where are they landing?" she asked.

"The only parking lot in town. Behind the bank."

"They'll have supplies for us?"

He nodded. "I'll take the gurney from the medical exam room. We'll heap the supplies on top of it and wheel it back."

"Shouldn't I help with moving the patients?"

"No. You're on suture detail. Others can help."

Grace hurried outside and grabbed Carmen to assist her. She watched Dr. Novak run to the landing site, leaving Petra still in charge. One chopper had landed and turned off the engine.

Dr. Novak talked to a rescue worker as several people unloaded items onto the gurney. He pointed at the triage area as Grace and Carmen took their first patient into the clinic.

Grace painstakingly sutured as Carmen assisted and translated when necessary. Dr. Novak's wound had been by far the worst of them. Throughout the procedures, they heard shouts and movement outside.

Dr. Novak had entered the clinic waiting room to drop off supplies but didn't interrupt her. They'd overheard his and Gabriel's conversation.

"They can only take four at a time. We need to quickly load these patients in triage order so the other chopper can land. That one has food and water," Dr. Novak said.

"Who's going?"

"The two in urgent status, and Señora Lopez and her husband."

"How many more need to go?" Gabriel asked.

"So far, only four more."

"Will more choppers come?"

"Yes." They moved boxes as they spoke, and then they left. Soon after, one chopper departed and the second one landed. Grace wondered why American Red Cross volunteers hadn't come. Maybe they took longer to mobilize.

"That's not so bad," Carmen said, as Grace unwrapped a man's haphazardly bandaged hand. The man winced.

Seeing his discomfort, Grace gave Carmen the secret signal to keep him distracted while she cleaned the wound. Carmen fired away, in Spanish, with her usual aplomb.

Several minutes later, the last patient had been sutured. Grace handed him the envelope with ibuprofen as Carmen explained in Spanish how to care for the wound.

"Carmen, thank you. Can you see if Petra's okay?"

"That was very exciting, Graciela. I will help you anytime."

"I couldn't have done it without you." Grace hugged her. "Ever since I arrived, you've been so kind to me. Thank you."

"You are special, Graciela. We are lucky the doctor brought you to us."

Grace enjoyed Carmen's motherly praise. Then she spotted their black travel cases beside the supply boxes. "I should restock these."

"I will let *el doctor* know where you are."

"Please tell him I'll be right out with fresh supplies."

"I will."

Grace hurried opening the boxes. She had rescued people today, then sutured patients by herself! She had actually made a difference. She'd never known if she'd really made a difference in anyone's life before.

As Grace completed refilling the travel cases, a sharp aftershock struck. The clinic building swayed and screeched. Shouts and screams from outside made her adrenaline rush. She grabbed the cases and rushed outside. The porch strained in protest.

The remaining chopper lifted into the air. They were on their own again.

"Grace!" Dr. Novak emerged from the crowd, concern etched in his expression.

"The cases are refilled," she said, hurrying down the steps to offer him the supplies and medicines. "Are there more patients?"

He stepped in front of her. "I wasn't worried about the cases."

She looked up at him. His gaze softened as he reached out and cupped her cheek. His touch mesmerized her.

"I was worried about you," he said.

"Me?" She recognized that look and held her breath. He couldn't possibly mean what his expression told her . . . that he truly cared.

He took the cases from her grasp and set them down. Their hands touched, and Grace's pulse pounded through her body. "Don't worry, Doctor. I can continue working."

"Take a break, Grace."

He'd said her name with such sweet seductiveness, she couldn't move. "What about Petra?"

"Mandy and her friends are giving Petra a break."

"How's Mandy's injury?" she asked.

"Petra doused it with alcohol, plastered a Band-Aid on it, and put her to work."

Grace smiled.

He reached into his pants' back pockets and pulled out two water bottles. "Sit." He sat on one of the cases. "Work crews are on their way by bus from Calexico."

"Great." Grace took a water and opened it. The liquid soothed her dry throat. She sat opposite him. He'd watched her every move.

"Congratulations. I'm giving you a promotion to Head

Nurse. The pay's the same, and there are no additional benefits."

"What?" She laughed.

"All I can offer you is the title, but you earned it." He clinked his water bottle against hers.

"I'm honored," she said. "You deserve a promotion too. May I suggest Director of Pediatrics?"

"I like it. I accept."

She clinked her bottle against his, and as they smiled, their gazes fused. Grace had never wanted to be kissed by a man more than she did at that moment. Had never wanted to reach out and bring a man closer to her. She'd happily accept his kisses as ample compensation for her promotion. And she'd more than willingly give hers to him, if he still wanted them.

Grace wiped a smudge from his face. He covered her hand with his and kissed her palm. Bolts of pleasure coursed through her. "Dr. Novak . . ."

"Ryan," he said hoarsely.

Just one kiss. What harm could come from one simple kiss? she thought.

He placed his hand under her chin, tilting her head back. A tremor passed through Grace at his touch, at this deliberate contact with her. His thumb traced her lips, and she closed her eyes to savor the electrifying sensation.

"Do you want me to kiss you?" he asked.

Grace held in a gasp. *Yes, of course. No, absolutely not.* His provocative question presented a point of no return. If they kissed, she would tumble in a tailspin toward disaster. She didn't want to want him. But didn't she already crave his kiss?

Grace opened her eyes. The tenderness of his expression took her breath away. She didn't have to tumble helplessly. She had some control. She could choose not to give her heart. Grace could kiss him and keep things casual between them.

She nodded.

"Tell me, Grace," he said. "I want to hear the words."

She swallowed hard. "Kiss me, Dr. Novak."

"Gladly." He brushed his lips across hers. A fire ignited within her, spreading through her body. He encircled her in his arms and deepened the kiss. Grace held on to him, wanting his kiss to continue forever.

I will not give my heart. She had a new mantra.

"Grace, I've wanted to kiss you since the day you arrived." His husky murmur caused a surge in her blood pressure.

She kissed his cheek. She could get used to having this man in her arms.

"Good thing I didn't know that," she said, caressing his jaw.

He took her face in his hands. "You know it now." He lowered his head and set her on fire once more.

His kiss stirred something deep inside her. Grace couldn't define it with him slowly exploring her mouth, deliciously unraveling her restraint. Ryan Novak gave of himself; he didn't just take.

"Dr. Novak . . . ," she said, breathlessly.

"Please call me Ryan."

"I can't."

"Can't what?"

"Call you anything but Dr. Novak."

"Since you make the name sound so nice, I guess it's okay."

Grace loved the sound of his raspy voice. And she loved the way he held on to her, as if she meant something to him.

But the way she felt in his arms didn't change her history. She had bad luck with doctors, and this one already enticed her too much. He even had her making up new mantras just so she could kiss him without guilt. They hadn't helped. Guilt engulfed her, and she realized with a rush of fresh humiliation that she wasn't equipped to handle a casual romantic liaison. She didn't have the stomach to lead a person on, make him think she cared when she did not. And she certainly wouldn't allow herself to care for him. If she didn't stop herself right now, he would persuade her to give more than she could. Then she'd be the one hurting, not Ryan Novak.

Be strong, Grace. It's the only way you'll survive.

Agonizingly, she writhed out of his embrace.

"Nothing can come of this. Tomorrow we must forget today ever happened," she said.

"Why?"

"Because I have to last a year, that's why," she said.

His expression changed. "You'll have to do better than that."

"I only want a professional relationship."

"You should have thought of that before you asked me to kiss you."

"I . . . I'm sorry." Remembering she'd brazenly invited him into her arms made Grace feel reprehensible. She had just wanted a taste. And she had expected him to be like all the other doctors in her past and be happy that there were no strings attached. Only Dr. Novak did not look happy.

"Running never solves anything, Grace."

"I'm not running!"

"Then you picked a hell of a time to make a decision."

"I'm sticking to it. I'm sorry if I . . ."

"Consider the entire event forgotten," he said.

As if Grace could forget.

But she had no choice. She had to keep this job for a year. If her own track record was anything to go by, then Dr. Novak would be ready for another woman in six months. That's when her husband had taken on his first girlfriend. What was rule number three? *Always remember, after all you gave your husband, it wasn't enough. You weren't enough.*

"You shouldn't ask a man to kiss you if you don't mean it, Grace. It makes him think . . ." Ryan stopped before making a fool of himself.

"I wasn't thinking," she said. "I won't make that mistake again."

Ryan's temple twitched. He didn't like his kiss being referred to as a *mistake*. "It was a mistake for me too," he brazenly lied.

He watched her face pale before she diverted her gaze. He felt like a jerk.

"I don't want you ever to worry about your job," he said honestly. But could Grace really kiss him the way she had if she still grieved over the loss of her husband?

Hell, no! Grace's all-consuming kiss had come from deep within her soul. And she had roused the nucleus of his. He wondered if she would ever trust him enough to let him kiss her again.

Someone shouted his name.

"Dr. Novak, come quickly," Poncho said, running from the triage area. "It's Father Sanchez."

Ryan and Grace jumped to their feet. He cast an apologetic glance at her as they ran with their cases.

Remorse tormented Grace as they followed Poncho. One kiss from Ryan, and she had craved more. As urgently as their patients needed medicines, she had felt the need for contact with Dr. Novak. She promptly condemned her overreaction to him and her brash request for his kiss. Thankfully, the moment had passed, and common sense had returned. She'd never ask Ryan Novak to kiss her again. But, heaven help her, she couldn't prevent herself from wanting him to.

Resist him, Grace. You don't believe in love anymore. And you certainly don't believe doctors' lies. Dr. Novak didn't want love either. If anything, he only wanted a fling. As she ran alongside him, Grace wished she believed all that.

Chapter Thirteen

Poncho led them to Father Sanchez, who was lying on the ground in the nearly demolished residential district.

"What was he doing out here?" Dr. Novak asked.

"We were reinforcing homes that were salvageable and pulling down what was too dangerous."

Grace's mind latched on to Poncho's words. Was her heart salvageable, or was attempting to love again too dangerous? She knew the answer. Her whole motivation for rushing to Mexico was to hide from shame *and* love.

Father Sanchez lay on the threshold of a corrugated tin house. He grasped his right shoulder with his left hand.

"Father, what happened?" Dr. Novak placed his fingers on the father's wrist, taking his pulse.

"I felt pain . . . can't move my arm." Father Sanchez's slurred speech and partial paralysis gave them clues. *"Mucho dolor."*

"Where's the pain, Father?" Dr. Novak checked the man's pupils with his penlight.

The right side of Father Sanchez's face drooped. "My . . . shoulder and my arm feel numb."

"Have you taken any medications?" Ryan pulled out his stethoscope. Grace loosened the Father's clothing.

"No, Doctor."

"Do you have dizziness?"

"*Sí.*"

Ryan slipped the stethoscope under the open collar and listened. "What were you doing before?"

Father Sanchez could not remember. The short-term memory loss added another symptom of a stroke.

"Are you allergic to anything?"

"No, Doctor. What is causing this?"

"You've probably had a stroke, Father," Dr. Novak said. "You'll be airlifted to the hospital tonight."

Grace already had a nasal cannula connected to the portable oxygen tank.

"One hundred percent," Dr. Novak said, positioning the cannula on the patient. "I wish I had a thrombolytic agent to administer to him." Instead he took the aspirin Grace handed him. He helped Father Sanchez sit up and swallow it.

Grace wrote on the tape and applied it to his chest.

"But I have work to do. I can't leave," Father Sanchez said.

"You've done too much already. Several volunteers are on their way to help. You get better. Believe me, there will be lots of work left to do when you return."

Grace's heart twisted at the way Dr. Novak patted Father Sanchez's hand soothingly, reassuring him that he would be fine.

"My church . . ."

"Don't worry, Father. We'll repair the church and the school."

"We can take him to the clinic in my truck," Poncho said.

"Thank you." Dr. Novak closed up the cases and carried them to the truck. "Grace, sit with Poncho. I'll ride in the back with Father Sanchez." The men gently hoisted the patient into the rear of the vehicle.

Upon their arrival at the triage area, Benita approached them.

"Doctor, there are some injured tourists you need to see."

"Hold on. Grace, can you get the gurney for Father Sanchez?"

"Of course." As Grace hustled to retrieve the gurney, she heard Dr. Novak talk to Benita.

"Show me," he said. She took his hand, and they weaved through victims sitting on the ground.

Grace wondered if Benita felt a bolt of lightning shoot through her body at Ryan's touch too. At that moment, Grace experienced a bolt of jealousy.

Brushing aside her irrational feelings, she settled Father Sanchez onto the gurney and took his vital signs. Grace monitored him continuously, making certain his symptoms didn't worsen.

"Bless you and *el doctor*," the Father said. "I see a light in your eyes you did not have before."

His slowly spoken words surprised Grace. "Working hard takes my mind off my problems, Father."

"Mourning the loss of a loved one is difficult."

Shame washed over Grace, and she leaned closer to him. "Father, I have a confession to make. . . ."

Another helicopter noisily landed, preventing further conversation. More supplies were off-loaded. And since all the patients could sit up in the small chopper, three patients and two parents were packed inside. Grace helped move Father Sanchez. Dr. Novak provided a report to the medics on each patient.

As the chopper lifted, the swooshing blades brought a welcome breeze but unwelcome dust and racket.

Then the noise intermingled with that of a large vehicle honking its horn behind them.

"The bus," Dr. Novak said.

Villagers gathered around the worn yellow school bus.

The door hissed open, and a group of six volunteers disembarked.

"I'm Dr. Novak. We're pleased to have your assistance."

"Dr. Jones. Sorry we took so long. We stopped at La Trinidad. They had many casualties," a man with a gray beard said. He introduced the five other volunteers.

"Where's the mayor?" a young man who looked like a bodybuilder asked.

"He left on a medevac chopper with a broken leg."

"The police chief?" the bus driver and male nurse asked.

"Working someplace. The water well, I think," Carmen said.

"What can we do?" Dr. Jones asked.

"The emergency patients have been treated. We're still getting stragglers, and I think tomorrow we'll need to visit the nearby villages. I'll let Poncho tell you about the infrastructure," Dr. Novak said.

"We've got an electrician and a civil engineer here." Dr. Jones pointed at the bodybuilder and a middle-aged man.

The group huddled around Dr. Novak and Poncho to assess what needed to be done. The sun had begun to set.

Grace rubbed her back. She guessed she had another two hours of work left in her before she fizzled.

"Many citizens were left homeless and are in the inn. We don't have decent accommodations for you," Dr. Novak said.

"We sleep in the bus. We brought canned food and water for you as well, but I admit, we gave some to the folks in La Trinidad," Dr. Jones said.

"We appreciate anything you can do," Dr. Novak said. Carmen, Gabriel, Poncho, and the others agreed. The revitalized group dispersed, ready to carry out their plans. Ryan found Grace and took her hand in his, catching her off guard.

"What's our next assignment?" she asked in a panicked tone. Why would he publicly hold her hand?

"I'm getting you off your feet."

"Excuse me?"

"You haven't eaten a thing all day. You haven't taken any breaks except that short one. . . ." His voice trailed off. "And I bet you're exhausted."

"I won't take a break until the others do," she said.

"Everyone has taken breaks. Several breaks."

"Not you."

"I'm taking mine with you," he said.

Grace's heart hammered. She had to tell him no more kissing, or talking about kissing. No more seductive glances or handholding. And they were to spend their off time apart.

"Where are we going?" Her voice sounded unnatural.

"Relax, Grace. I'm taking you to the cantina for a meal."

"Oh." She couldn't keep the quaver out of the one word.

"Then I'm taking you to bed."

"Dr. Novak . . ."

Inside the cantina he released her hand, temporarily confusing her. Carmen and Gabriel's eldest daughter, Inez, waved him over. They talked briefly. She pointed behind her, and he rubbed his hands together and nodded.

Grace sat and suddenly felt weary. Her back ached. Her neck hurt. And there in front of her Ryan Novak had the audacity to appear refreshed. He smiled as he sat down across from her.

"They've been serving everyone rice and bean burritos. But we're getting chicken in ours. They set aside fresh fruit for us too."

"That was considerate of Carmen."

"She really likes you," he said, watching Grace closely.

"I like her too."

He rose, moving behind her, and before she could protest, he began massaging her shoulders.

Instead of swatting him away, instead of admonishing him, she moaned in pleasure. She closed her eyes, wishing she could sleep right there. His hands kneaded her tired muscles and sent blissful shivers through her.

Forgetting about food, she longed to lean her body against him. Would he continue caressing her? If she faced him, would he see her hunger for him?

"Here's your dinner," Inez said.

"*Muchas gracias.* We're famished," he said.

Grace took a moment to comprehend why Dr. Novak had stopped the massage. "Oh. Thank you, Inez."

Grace forgot all her table manners and ate ravenously.

Dr. Novak seemed amused but ate with as much gusto as she.

Inez brought them a pitcher of water, when Benita burst in.

"There's a group of ten headed this way. Those volunteers and your family," Benita said to Inez, as she glanced at Dr. Novak and Grace.

"Do you need help?" Grace asked Inez.

"No," Dr. Novak said.

Inez and Benita chuckled. "Thank you but no," Inez said. The two women left for the kitchen.

"Eat up. One never knows when the next meal may come."

Grace frowned at him. "I'm capable of cooking."

"I saw what happened the last time you went behind Carmen's stove."

Grace groaned. "Aren't you going to let me forget that?"

"How about a deal? You stop taunting me about the contest, and I may consider not bringing up your cooking prowess."

"Deal," she said, too tired to argue.

"Besides, I insist that you rest."

"Fine. But I insist that you rest as well."

The noisy group entered the cantina.

Dr. Novak stood. "Good idea. Let's go." He escorted her out a door through the kitchen.

Grace saw Benita hold on to a wall and sway.

"What's wrong?" she asked.

"Too much shaking. It makes me dizzy."

"Aftershocks can have that affect," Dr. Novak said.

Benita nodded. *"Buenas noches." Good night.*

Outside, the moon shone brightly.

"Is that a good sign or a bad sign after an earthquake?" Grace asked.

"A full moon is always a good sign," he said with a wink.

She rolled her eyes at him.

They neared La Clínica Pediátrica. It had sustained damage but held firm. "When Poncho rented me this building, he said it was one of the few town structures that was solidly built."

"He's a man of his word," Grace said, as they climbed the steps. She turned on the lights. They still worked. Inside, things looked worse than what they were.

Papers were scattered everywhere, boxes torn open, broken glass and furniture strewn about.

"I know what you're thinking. The answer is no," he said.

"You're clairvoyant now?"

"We'll clean up tomorrow." Ryan ushered her down the hallway to their bedrooms.

She stopped at her door. A rush of guilt hit her. Dr. Novak had looked after her throughout the hectic night. He had looked after everyone but himself. She glanced at his sleeve. "How's your injury?"

"Thanks to you, I'm good as new." His gaze met hers.

As tirelessly as he worked, she wanted to do more for him. He needed a few moments of someone nurturing *him*. "You must be worn out and achy. At least let me give you a massage."

Even she caught the reluctance in her tone.

"You sound so eager," he said wryly. Standing at his threshold, he flicked on his light switch.

Grace pushed him into his room, seeing it for the first

time. The mess made her forget her embarrassment about offering to massage the last man she should be massaging.

"Did it look like this before the quake?"

"Like what?"

He sat on a chair at a small desk. Grace dug into his shoulders, determined to give him a deep-tissue massage so as not to caress him.

His satisfied moan excited her.

"Ah . . . Grace . . . you have magical hands."

"Try to relax. Your muscles are so tight." She massaged his shoulders, upper arms, and neck. All the while he made noises like a man experiencing great pleasure. She had to bite her tongue and focus on the clothes strewn about the floor, ignoring her desire to rub her hands across his chest.

"Does your arm hurt?"

"I forgot all about it," he said. "Wait a sec." He slipped his shirt off over his head.

Grace sharply inhaled. His sculpted muscles tempted her.

"Go ahead." He sounded tired.

The spasm of guilt returned. He just wanted a massage for his aching muscles, nothing more. He'd worked tenaciously for hours, helping so many. He deserved a few minutes of her attention.

When her hands made contact with his skin, a delectable yearning awakened within her. She fought the impulse to bend and kiss his shoulder. She suppressed a whimper of frustration. Why couldn't they have met a year from now? Perhaps by then her heart would have healed. By then her backbone would have stiffened, and she'd be mentally ready for . . . for what? She'd never be ready for heartbreak again. Determined to prevail, Grace dug deeper. Her arms ached.

"I suppose my second cooking lesson is canceled tomorrow night," she said.

"Grace . . ." He placed his hands over hers and tugged her into his lap. "Stop tormenting me."

She gasped. "I . . . I thought you liked it."

"I love your touch. But I want more." He stroked her cheek. His other hand curved around her waist. "Isn't this where we left off?" His gaze was full of longing.

Words escaped Grace as her senses reeled.

"It's where I want you, in my arms," he said. He brushed his lips across hers.

Her blood sizzled.

"Dr. Novak . . . ," she whispered, reaching up and clasping her hands around his neck. Grace could no longer fight her attraction. She planted kisses across his cheek and slowly across his shoulder.

He shuddered. "Yes, Grace."

She spread her hands over his chest and shoulders and touched him the way she'd been craving to ever since she first glimpsed him.

"You're driving me wild." He held on to her as he stood. In one fluid movement he sat her on the desk. Gazing into her eyes, he dropped his hands to his sides.

You can never be enough for him, a voice inside her warned.

But the warmth Grace saw in his eyes eased her sense of inadequacy.

"You're beautiful," he said.

At that moment, Grace truly felt beautiful. She smiled at him.

Ryan leaned down and gave her a kiss. He gave a piece of himself, focusing completely on her.

Breathless, she pulled away. And just as quickly she yearned for his touch.

"Grace, do you trust me?" He cupped her face. "It feels so right to me."

His conviction chased away most of her doubts. It felt right to her too. And she was only here for a year. He couldn't hurt her if she knew when it would end.

"I want to," she said. "I want it to be right."

"Thank you, Grace."

Her heart pounded as he tenderly kissed her. "Ryan . . ."

"Yes, darling." His mouth teased her lips.

Grace circled her legs around his waist, trapping him. "You can't get away."

"Believe me, I don't want to get away," he said, his voice hoarse.

His words encouraged her.

He looked at her the way he had before, with genuine tenderness and affection. Grace ached for him. And at that moment, she realized she loved him.

The notion hit her harder than the earthquake had.

He paused, as if waiting to hear her declaration.

"You're the woman for me," he whispered.

Every touch, every kiss, conveyed his fondness for her.

She wanted him to feel her affection for him, as he had shown her. And she wanted him to feel her love. She kissed his cheek as she massaged his shoulders.

He shuddered. "Grace, oh, my . . ."

"Ryan . . ." She caught herself before blurting out, *I love you.* Instead she laid her head against his chest.

Feeling his heartbeat against her cheek, Grace felt whole again.

She snuggled into his embrace. "I'm too cozy to move."

"Me too."

She relished the feel of him holding her tightly.

"I'd like the contest Web site address. I'm ready to cast my vote," she said. She felt his deep chuckle along her front.

"For anyone I know?"

"Definitely."

"Don't make any promises. You haven't seen the other candidates," he said.

"I've made my decision, and I can't be swayed."

He caressed her hair and kissed her head. "Grace, stay with me forever."

Her heart stopped beating. And her joy came to an abrupt end.

Chapter Fourteen

Ryan felt Grace's body tense for a moment. Not the reaction he'd expected.

"I'll clean my room," he teased, wanting her to relax again.

She remained silent and still, and finally he noted her steady breathing.

"Grace?"

The even rise and fall of her shoulders told him she'd fallen asleep in his arms. His loins tightened at the memory of her kissing him, her hands caressing him.

"Sleep tight, my angel." He gently lifted her, not wanting to wake her. He kissed her head as he carried her to her room. Her scent teased his nostrils. He inhaled deeply, and visions of his precious Grace enchanting him with her kisses filled his mind. He felt humbled by her selflessness. But of all the extraordinary things she'd given him, the one that affected him most of all was her trust.

He perceived that trust was not something Grace gave

easily or often. Somehow he'd earned it, and he vowed never to lose it. He covered her with the bedspread and planted a soft kiss on her cheek. Back in his own room, he drifted off, dreaming of Grace.

When Grace awoke, she spontaneously reached out. The empty space beside her felt cold. She had cuddled and fallen asleep in Ryan's arms. But not before Ryan had asked the impossible.

But he didn't mean really forever. He couldn't possibly. She knew he'd only meant for her full year.

Without a doubt, Grace recognized she loved Ryan Novak fully and completely. She smiled, enjoying the lift to her spirit. Ryan regarded her with admiration and courtesy. Naturally he'd win her love. But twelve months later, despite how Grace felt, she'd leave alone. That truth scared her. But wouldn't not loving him hurt far worse?

Outside, the sound of hammers and drills and saws startled her. She sat up. *The earthquake!* She'd forgotten about the earthquake. The villagers were already hard at work.

A soft knock on the door sounded.

"I brought you breakfast," Ryan said.

Grace sprang out of bed. "Why didn't you wake me?" As she cracked open the door, her heart flipped.

He hadn't shaved yet, and his hair was a bit ruffled, making him look far more sumptuous than the tray of food he was carrying.

"You deserved to sleep in." He entered and kissed her cheek. His whiskers tickled her face.

"Thank you." She sat on the bed. "Join me for breakfast?" she asked shyly.

He smiled. "Since I haven't eaten yet, I'd love to." He lifted a ceramic plate covering a dish of huevos rancheros, chorizo, and *papas*. He took the fork and scooped up a morsel of egg. But instead of taking the bite, he brought the fork to her mouth. Grace accepted it. He took turns with the fork until the breakfast of zesty eggs, spicy sausage, and potatoes disappeared. With each bite, their gazes had met, and it seemed that each time his gaze smoldered a bit more than before. "Drink your juice," he said, rising.

"Am I the last person in town to wake up?"

"No one's checking." He set the tray aside and sat back on the edge of the bed.

Grace longed to rub her cheek against his.

He entwined her hand with his, bringing them down to his lap. "Grace," he murmured. "Tell me you're mine." He studied her now, as if he worried what her answer might be.

His word choice threw her. Hadn't she come to Mexico seeking independence? She'd lose that if she became *his*. "Can we take this one day at a time?"

"No," he said.

Grace blinked. "What do you mean, no?"

"That's not the kind of partnership I want with you."

She bit her lip. *It's all I can offer,* she thought. But she might consider offering more to this man. "What do you want?"

He shook his head. "What do *you* want from me?"

True love. Fidelity. A relationship where I keep my self-respect. Her list went on. Her requests had proved too much to ask. At least that's what Grace's husband had apparently felt.

Suddenly Grace panicked. She didn't want this relationship to end up like her marriage. Hadn't her husband been a thoughtful, courteous man before they married? Somehow Grace had changed him, turned him into an unfaithful and shallow person. What if she did that to Ryan?

"Honesty," she said.

Tilting his head, he studied her. "That's a given. Isn't it?"

She kept silent. The ruckus outside grew, a hint that others had more urgent problems than hers.

"That's it? That's all you want from me?" Annoyance tinged his voice.

"It's important," she said.

He rubbed his jaw, waiting for her to continue. "I require your honesty too."

Grace bunched the bedspread in her fists. She didn't want to reveal her feelings. "I'd like to slow down. I'm not ready for"—she summoned her courage—"for being a couple." In hindsight, she did better alone. Being a couple caused her grief. Grace didn't want another romance that dissolved faster than the sutures she applied.

Ryan tucked a finger under her chin and raised her gaze to meet his. "I want you, but not until you're ready and know how much you mean to me."

His words accelerated her pulse. "You want me?"

"That's right. I want all or nothing, Grace." His voice strengthened, emphasizing his words. "In return, I'll give you my all."

Her heart soared. She could live with that. Even for

just a year. That was more than she'd gotten in the past. No one had given her his all before. Grace opened her mouth to speak.

He exhaled. "I understand . . . naturally you're still hurting from your loss. . . . I can't begin to imagine the pain of losing a spouse." He shook his head. "Of course it's too soon for being a couple, at least in public. We can slow down," he said.

He swept his mouth across hers, tenderly sealing his promise.

Her thoughts swirled. He presumed that she still loved her husband. Did she?

They both heard the door to the clinic open.

"Doctor?" Jaime's voice called.

By nine in the morning, Ryan and Grace had checked Jaime's wounds and removed the Steri Strips, swept up more glass and debris from the floors, and begun making minor repairs. They'd been interrupted by villagers who stopped in for a fresh bandage or reassurance by the doctor.

"Why don't you sift through yesterday's records and see who we need to make house calls on? Dr. Jones agreed to see any new patients today." Ryan had a tool kit spread out on the waiting-room floor.

"Can you repair that flooring yourself?"

"I think so. It's not too bad. Only one floorboard needs replacing." He rose from his hands and knees. "I'll see if the guys outside have a piece of wood they can spare."

She smiled as he stepped out. Grace didn't doubt the villagers would hand over whatever the doctor wanted.

Dr. Novak was a household name in this town. She glanced at him through the broken window.

And he was hers. *If* she was willing to take a chance. An all-or-nothing chance. Butterflies fluttered in her stomach.

She sorted through the jumbled records in a heap on the desk. They'd tossed them there when cleaning the floor. Most of them didn't even have folders. "Might as well do this right," she said, walking to Ryan's office.

She opened his file cabinet, searching for empty folders. In the bottom drawer she found them. She retrieved a stack and returned to the waiting room.

Opening the top folder, she gasped. Inside were letters addressed to Ryan from several different women. The postmarks were current. In fact all of them were from this week. "What the heck?" Despite her better judgment, Grace opened one and read it. The explicit words unsettled her.

"Fan mail." Why would Ryan keep these? She denied the obvious answers. He enjoyed reading them. He intended to contact these women. He had already contacted these women.

But Carmen and the others teased him about his fan mail. He didn't take any of it seriously, did he? He surely hadn't shared these letters with Carmen.

She peeked into the remaining folders. They were all empty. She stuffed the letters back into the folder and marched it back into Ryan's office. The other folders in the drawer didn't have fan mail in them. Grace straightened and glanced around. Where were the tons of letters Carmen claimed existed?

Why did she care? Why did they bother her? *Shake it*

off. Grace did not wish to acknowledge she'd become that distrustful. Who needed a suspicious woman in his life? Not Ryan Novak. She exited the office and faced the storage closet. *Aha.*

Unable to stop herself, she opened it. To the left of their emergency medical cases sat a stack of three cardboard boxes. Grace lifted the lid on the top one. "There you are." A mound of letters filled the box. Grace had seen enough. She closed the box, wishing she could stuff her cynicism away in the dark closet.

Couldn't she laugh about the letters, as Mandy had? Ryan hadn't refuted their existence. *It's not like he's hiding anything from you,* she told herself. Grace found herself back at the table in the waiting room. *He's done nothing to rationalize your absurd behavior.*

Outside the clinic, the rescue volunteers had joined Ryan's conversation with the villagers. She heard his laugh, and her belly fluttered once more. Everything would be all right. Later, she'd mention his fan mail. Perhaps he'd tell her something that made her laugh too.

"Excuse me."

Grace spun to see Benita standing at the door. "Oh, I didn't hear you. Come in." She glanced at the appointment calendar. "Do you have an appointment?"

"No. But can you squeeze me in, please?"

"Of course, Benita." Grace poised a pencil over the calendar. "What is the purpose of your visit?"

Benita didn't answer. Instead she glanced at her wringing hands. "I need to talk to Ryan."

Her use of his first name surprised Grace. "He'll be right back. I'm sure . . ."

They heard his footsteps on the steps outside.

"Look what I got." He held a piece of floorboard almost identical to the clinic's. Then he saw their visitor.

"Benita. *Buenos días,*" Ryan said cheerfully. "You were amazing yesterday."

Benita looked comforted. "Thanks. You and Grace are legends now."

Ryan smiled at Grace. "Guess what? See that nice yellow bus out there? It could soon be ours!"

"Really? How on earth did you manage that, and without a poker game?" Grace asked.

"I told Dr. Jones about some grant possibilities. He can get a new bus for his type of organization. He didn't know about the grant for vehicles, which encourages donation of the used vehicle to a charity or school. He says if he gets it, we can have their old bus."

"I can help with the grant application," Grace said enthusiastically.

"Wow!" Benita said.

"Oh, Benita's asked if you can see her before your next patient arrives," Grace said.

"Absolutely," he said without hesitation. "We've fixed up both exam rooms." He set the floorboard aside, then put his hand on the small of Benita's back, guiding her to the room they'd just cleaned. Benita glanced at him adoringly.

Initial consultations with the doctor were private. So Grace watched the door to the exam room close. A mixture of feelings pelted her, but she immediately brushed off the twinge of possessiveness that nipped at her.

What's wrong with me? Grace agonized. *I've never felt this insecure before.*

Her distasteful emotions had no place in the clinic and were completely unacceptable. Benita had a right to consult the doctor without worrying about a jealous nurse.

Grace busied herself with the schedule of patients. The calendar had two names she could cross off. Those were patients who had been airlifted to Mexicali. Jaime had already been seen, leaving them with three more patients. The load had been left light to allow for immunizations at the school. Now they could use that time to make house calls and finish repairing the clinic.

They would work all day and night helping repair the village as well. At least there were some things she and Ryan Novak had in common. A devotion to helping others, the ability to work tirelessly, and a strong sense of responsibility to the profession. She'd seen dedication before, but Dr. Novak went far above and beyond. She felt herself unwinding.

Grace heard a woman crying. *Benita?*

Yes, the weeping came from the exam room. It could be anything. Grace felt helpless. She remembered seeing Benita in the cantina. Once she had witnessed Benita's lightheadedness. Another time the woman had complained of having the flu. Now Grace wondered if these were symptoms of something far more serious. Benita was too young and beautiful to suffer a life-threatening illness. Grace prayed for her.

The door opened. "Grace," Ryan called.

She hurried into the room. Benita sat on the exam table. Her makeup had smeared from her tears.

"When's our next patient due?"

"Not for an hour. Jorge is in Mexicali." Grace handed Benita a tissue.

"Good. I need your assistance." He glanced at her oddly. "Prepare the patient for an exam."

"What kind of exam?" Grace sensed his discomfort.

"The gown, Grace." He spoke abnormally tightly as he brushed past her, leaving the women alone.

Grace stared at the door.

"I think I may have upset him with my news," Benita said.

The words cued Grace that Benita needed the doctor's attention, and she nabbed a paper gown from a drawer. "Please remove all your clothing. Wear this with the opening in the front."

Benita nodded and began undressing.

"Do you need help?"

"I can manage." Benita said quietly.

Grace put a blue plastic towel on the steel tray and set down items the doctor required for a pelvic exam. She could easily grab whatever else he needed.

Benita hopped back onto the gurney table.

"Lie down, please." Grace spread a drape over her.

Dr. Novak returned. He avoided looking at Grace as he slipped on gloves.

"A pediatric clinic doesn't have all the adult equipment," he said to Benita, referring to the absence of stirrups.

Grace helped keep Benita's legs from slipping.

"If it's what we suspect, this will just take a minute."

"Okay."

Ryan was not himself. Grace had a bad feeling, and her worry for Benita increased. She fought the urge to hold Benita's hand.

Ryan completed the exam. "Let her get dressed," he said on his way out.

Grace assisted Benita off the table. She refused to look at Benita's face, afraid of letting Benita see what was in her expression.

Instead Grace ripped the tissue paper off the exam table and shoved it into the trash. The doctor hadn't taken any swab cultures.

"Are you not feeling well?" Benita asked.

"I'm concerned about you," Grace said.

"Don't be. Dr. Novak will take care of me."

"Yes. He'll be right back," Grace said, as she slipped out of the room.

In the hallway, Ryan leaned his back and head against the wall. He seemed drained of energy, with no trace remaining of the enthusiastic man who had gone searching for a piece of wood only minutes earlier. He said nothing as his gaze remained fixed straight ahead.

"Give her a minute," Grace said, as uncertainty crept into her. One reason a doctor performed a pelvic exam was to confirm pregnancy. Grace wondered if this was the case.

"Thank you."

"Shall I go in with you?"

"No," he said.

Grace had never seen Ryan like this, and her concern evolved into fear. "I'll be here, if you need me."

Ryan straightened and rapped on the door before entering. He closed the door behind him.

Grace remained planted in the hallway. Suspicion gnawed at her insides. She had never eavesdropped on a doctor and his patients before. But something compelled her to stay at the door and listen. Her heart thudded as her apprehension rose.

"You were right. You are pregnant," he said.

Benita sobbed.

Grace heard Ryan's soothing words and deduced he hugged Benita on the other side of the door.

"You once offered to marry me, remember?" Benita said. "Well, I accept."

Chapter Fifteen

Grace felt herself sway.

"Dear Benita, I wish I could marry you. But I can't."

"I would make a good wife."

"Yes, I know you would."

Grace's heart felt as heavy as lead.

"My parents would approve of your proposal."

"Benita, I can't propose. I'm with Grace now."

"I didn't know." She wept. "I'm scared."

Ryan comforted her and muttered more soothing words that Grace couldn't understand.

Her mind reeled.

Ryan had once asked Benita to marry him!

Was Ryan the father of Benita's baby? If so, why wouldn't he marry her? How could he turn his back on the mother of his child just because another woman had entered his life?

Her stomach twisted and churned so much that Grace thought she would vomit. Maybe Ryan wasn't the honorable man she thought him to be. Had she been wrong yet again?

Unable to bear hearing more, she stumbled into the bathroom. She splashed cold water on her face. Ryan himself had said he wished he could marry Benita. Grace would not stand in their way. She couldn't live with herself, knowing another woman and her child needed him more than she did.

So what if Grace loved him, and so what if Ryan cared for her? His future family had priority over a temporary affair.

Her questions smashed into each other. Had Ryan really proposed marriage to Benita before? He hadn't denied it. When had they broken up? Why had they parted? Now that she thought about it, Grace recalled the two had always been extremely amicable toward each other. Perhaps they would have reunited if Grace hadn't entered the picture.

The only thing for her to do was promptly leave the picture. She grabbed a towel, surprised she hadn't shed a tear. There were worse reasons to break up than a man discovering he'd left a previous girlfriend pregnant.

Reasons Grace knew personally.

Thinking of her late husband, Grace scowled at her reflection in the mirror. If only she'd found out about his adultery before he had the wreck and died. She would have saved herself so much grief. Well, this time she would spare herself the misery. This time she'd break up. If she did so immediately, at least one of them could find happiness.

Grace tossed the towel into the sink. She spun and marched outside for a brisk walk.

As she passed the exam-room window, she saw Benita and Ryan wrapped tightly in each other's arms.

The ground beneath her seemed to shake.

After Benita left, Ryan searched for Grace for twenty minutes. Her walking out on him during a patient's visit was so out of character, it had him baffled.

He spotted her at the general store. Grace and other volunteers were repairing a wall. She hammered nails into the lumber with ferocity.

"Grace," he called, sensing something was wrong.

Her gaze met his, and the sadness he saw in her eyes confirmed his hunch.

"*Buenos días, Doctor,*" Poncho and the others said.

"*Buenos días,*" he replied, as he approached her. "Grace. We had a patient scheduled. Why did you leave?"

"You and Benita needed time alone."

He arched an eyebrow. "What makes you say that?"

She shrugged.

"I think they can do without you here. Let's go." He turned to Poncho. "I need to take my nurse away from you," he shouted.

"*Gracias, Señora Grace!*" Poncho waved at her.

She smiled and waved back, handing the hammer to Gabriel.

"What's up, Grace?" Ryan asked as they walked in silence back to the clinic.

"Do you have anything to tell me?" she asked.

He glanced at her. "About today's schedule?"

"About anything important, Ryan. Tell me now."

He followed her up the steps into the clinic, but he felt miles apart. She had something going on in her head, and he had no clue what it was. "What's on your mind?"

"I asked for honesty, remember?"

"I've always given you that." He paused. "But I'm not sure you've been completely honest with me. Have you?"

No, she hadn't. How could she be, when she hadn't even been honest with herself?

His cell phone rang in his pocket. "Damn." He retrieved it and glanced at the blinking number. "It's Mexicali. I have to take this."

"Of course." She knew that the doctors treating the San Felipe villagers might need crucial medical histories.

"Novak here." He listened. "Yes. Give me a second to locate her chart."

He hurried into his office. "Has Señora Lopez had a CT scan yet?" His voice trailed off.

For the first time, Grace did not have the urge to run but the need to talk. The need to explain to Ryan why she wasn't the woman for him—before he ruined his shot with Benita.

She waited impatiently. *Please hurry before I lose my nerve.*

The clinic door opened, and Benita entered, holding a plastic bottle. She smiled at Grace.

"I'm pleased you're here," Benita said. Her face did not glow with the elation that Grace had expected.

Grace tried to smile back, but her facial muscles refused. "How can I help you, Benita?" she said. Her gaze lowered to the woman's belly.

Suddenly Grace felt overwhelmed. She rushed to Benita and hugged her, unable to stop her tears. At least Ryan had picked a sweet, strong woman like Benita instead of one of those frivolous fans of his. Grace had once wondered what sort of a woman could keep Ryan happy. Surely Benita could.

Benita returned the hug. "Did Dr. Novak tell you?" she said, wiping away her own tears.

"No. I figured it out myself." Grace smiled at her now. "I'm only here until my contract expires, but if I can help you in any way, let me know." It dawned on Grace that the baby's delivery would occur while she still lived in San Felipe.

"Thank you." Benita held up the bottle. "I opened this and discovered these enormous pills. I can't swallow them."

Grace took the container. "Prenatal vitamins. You'll have to grind them like you do the chili peppers to make salsa."

"That's a good idea."

"What's a good idea?" Ryan asked Grace.

She spun to face him.

"Why did you give me such large pills?" Benita asked.

"Because there are a lot of things in there that you need." He glanced at Grace, trying to read her expression.

"I will have to grind one each day."

"Make sure you swallow all of it," he said.

"Yes, Doctor." Benita hugged Grace and left.

Grace looked expectantly at him. "If you want time off, I can show Dr. Jones which patients need a visit," she said.

"I don't need time off." He approached her. "We were interrupted in the middle of an important conversation." He noticed she wrung her hands as she took a step backward.

He stopped.

Finally she met his gaze. "Ryan, I . . ."

"You what?" he said too tautly.

"When I arrived in San Felipe, I was in mourning . . . but I was also in denial. You sensed I was hiding something, and you were right."

The news hit him like a punch in the gut. "What were you hiding?"

"My husband died in a car accident."

"I know." Is that what she was in denial about?

Ryan watched her body tense. She curled her palms into fists and raised her chin. The firm set of her lips and the edge in her voice told him that Grace had suffered more than the loss of her husband.

"I'm sorry." He braced himself, waiting for her to continue.

"Me too. That's when I found out he'd been having an affair. They shared a secret apartment . . . a love nest. He and my co-worker, Janet. They died together."

Ryan wished he could erase her pain. "Grace, how devastating for you." He reached for her, wanting to hold her, but she backed away.

"I made the arrangements for the funeral and carried on as any grieving wife would." She paused. "Going through his things, I found mementos from a medical conference he'd gone to a year before. He'd shared the room with a female doctor he'd worked with. From photos I uncovered, I'd say they shared the bed as well."

Ryan understood why Grace didn't trust men, especially doctors. He wished he could throttle her irresponsible husband.

"We were married for two years. He had at least two

affairs in those two years." She bit her lip. "In retrospect there were clues of other women, but I guess I'll never know for sure."

What kind of an idiot would look at another woman when he had Grace? Now Ryan's hands curled into fists.

"I donated everything I owned and ran away to Mexico. I didn't want to find or hear more evidence of his unfaithfulness. I'd been so stupid."

"You can't blame yourself."

"I do blame myself for not listening to the gossip. Everyone knew but me. I thought we were happily married. But apparently not."

"You hid that you were hurting from being deceived?"

"I not only hid the fact that my husband betrayed me, I ran from the truth. I ran from admitting that I was a failure as a wife. I don't know why he didn't ask for a divorce."

"I'm certain you were a wonderful wife. You can't let his flaws continue hurting you." Ryan didn't think Grace heard his assertions.

She paced as she spoke. "You know why I worked a few months on this ward and a few months on that ward? I moved on when the gossiping became unbearable. My husband blew off the rumors, and I believed him."

"Grace." Again he attempted to hold her.

She crossed her arms, halting him. "I'm only telling you this so you'll know why I'm severing our personal relationship."

"What?" Her words crashed down on him.

"I refuse to be with a man on unequal terms. Somewhere there's a man who wants only me. Like Gabriel and Carmen or Poncho and Petra. I deserve that too. It's not an unreasonable request. It's simple, really."

He opened his mouth to speak.

"That man is not you."

"What the hell did I do? Last night we were great. This morning we agreed to slow down. Now you're saying you want nothing to do with me? Are you leaving San Felipe?"

"No. I have a contract, and I'll fulfill my commitment for the year."

"Didn't *we* make a commitment?" Ryan stared at her, completely confused. It seemed as though he had missed out on a conversation or argument or something.

"I'm releasing you from that commitment," she said.

His agitation rose. "If we're supposed to be equal, why are you the only one making the decisions?" he snapped. "Maybe I don't want to be released from anything!"

Her eyes widened.

"Your husband was a jerk. I'd never cheat on a woman, let alone my wife! Don't compare me to that rat." Ryan knew he wasn't being reasonable. Of course she'd be leery of involvement after what she'd been through. He should be patient. She'd already said he was moving too fast for her.

"Give us a chance," he said, suddenly realizing he couldn't go back to being merely colleagues with her. That would tear him up . . . because he knew she loved him. Grace wore her heart on her sleeve. That was one of the things he loved about her.

Love?

He might as well admit it. *All or nothing,* he thought.

"I won't let you do this. You're punishing the wrong person. You weren't the failure; your ex was."

Grace's shoulders slumped. She looked awful, so sad.

"Let me give you the love you want," he said. "I do love you, Grace." He gathered her in his arms.

She sank into him for a moment. "What about Benita?"

"Huh?"

"I'm done with sharing a man. I couldn't do it. And you wouldn't be happy with me."

"Are you worried about sharing me with my career?" That made no sense whatsoever.

She stepped out of his embrace. "I'm stronger now. Wiser too. Why jump into a situation that's doomed to fail? Go with Benita."

"I never doubted your strength or your intelligence. But right now I'm doubting your sanity. What are you implying, and what does any of this have to do with Benita?"

Her gaze narrowed on him. "I overheard." Grace bit her lip. "I know about the baby."

He stared at her, unsure why this information troubled her. He waited for her to continue. "And?"

"I know you and she were together."

Comprehension finally hit him. "Grace. I thought you trusted me." Could her trust in him have faded so quickly?

"I do." The vulnerability she worked hard to conceal surfaced. "I know that whatever happened between you two ended before I arrived. I'm not accusing you of cheating on me. But Benita needs you now."

His nerves tightened. "You obviously overheard a different conversation than the one I participated in."

She crossed her arms and raised her chin.

Ryan was both proud of Grace and annoyed with her. Proud that she had the courage to stand her ground. But annoyed that she thought he could leave his own child fatherless.

He exhaled and planted his hands on her shoulders. "Let me rephrase that. You misunderstood whatever you heard. Benita and I have never been together."

"But she said you proposed to her."

He arched his eyebrows. "Didn't anyone ever tell you that nothing good comes from eavesdropping?"

"Explain why you didn't deny it."

He smiled. "I guess I did sort of propose to Benita."

Grace did not return his smile. Her face had paled.

"Benita was the first person from San Felipe to attend a university. Getting accepted was a major accomplishment. But Carmen told me Benita was considering dropping out after two years. I tried every pep talk I could think of to keep her in school. When she came home during summer break, she saw Carmen and some tourists admiring my Web site photos. Benita teased me about them, saying what a good catch I was, and I told her I would marry her if she got her degree. She assured me she would return to college."

Grace blinked. "That's it?"

"That's it. I am not the father of her baby."

Grace choked back a sob. Her eyes filled with tears. "I thought . . . I didn't want to break up a family."

"I understand. But I'm stunned you'd give up on us so easily."

"It was not easy," she whispered. "Working beside you for eleven and a half months would not have been easy."

No. That would take fortitude, he agreed.

"I went through hell when I found out my family had been torn apart. I could not do that—harm a family—especially people I cared for."

"So you thought it best to dump me?"

"It was a painful recourse. I swear I would have fought for you if there weren't a baby involved. Please don't think I'm a wimp who runs at the first sign of trouble."

Ryan wiped the loose hair from her face. "I've seen nothing but courage from you, darling. You're the last person I'd call a wimp."

"You must think I'm a buffoon, then."

"A snoop maybe." He put his hand under her chin and raised her gaze to his. "You were willing to sacrifice your happiness for someone else's. I can't stay mad about that. I'm thankful you confronted me instead of running away."

"I'm through with running away from my problems."

"Good. Because I don't want you to leave."

"Until my year is up?"

"Not ever." He noticed her eyes widen in bona fide surprise. "Don't you know how special you are?" he asked.

She shook her head. Ryan cupped her face in his hands. "You're caring, smart, determined, gutsy. Did I mention hot?"

She smiled.

"You're everything I could wish for, Grace."

"Me?"

"Yes, you."

"I only became those things by coming here, by meeting you."

"No. Those aspects of you were always there."

She reached up and caressed his cheek. "You bring out the best in me, Dr. Novak."

She did the same for him. She brought out his best too.

"I've been let down myself," Ryan said. "I was engaged once. My fiancée didn't want to leave the US and all its amenities. Instead she hooked up with another doctor and stayed behind."

"I don't believe it. She's crazy."

"It's just as well. I have no use for a wimpy wife, then or now."

"Now I understand your distaste for prima donnas."

"Don't be sad for me. She did me a favor," he said, smiling.

"You're rather cool about it."

"Don't get me wrong. I went through the hurt and anger. But I figure I'm lucky she betrayed me before we got married."

"I wasn't so lucky," Grace said.

"Sorry. I didn't mean to disrespect your marriage."

"You didn't. My husband did."

"I'm not like him."

"I know."

"I love you, Grace, and I want you to marry me."

She gasped. "Ryan, I think I fell in love with you the moment I saw you walk into the clinic with those wet trunks and flip-flops."

"Is that so?" He kissed her forehead.

She nodded. "I love you with all my heart."

Hearing Grace's words of love filled him with hope.

"But I'm afraid I did some other snooping," she

confessed. "Would you explain why you had fan letters in a folder in your cabinet?"

"You went through my file cabinet?" Purposeful snooping seemed hugely out of character for her.

"I needed empty folders for our new patients."

That sounded reasonable. Poor Grace, if she'd read the last one he had. "Those were the newest letters that arrived. I only opened one when you entered the office, and I shoved them into the folder."

"Do you answer them?" She placed her hands on her hips.

He smiled. "No. At my brother's suggestion, I open them to see if there's a check for the clinic. As you know, the clinic is a nonprofit, and I have Chad's instructions not to toss any of the letters, so we can send each fan a thank-you letter asking for a donation."

Grace was a good judge of character after all. "They're your mailing list. I knew there was a logical explanation."

He circled his arms around her. "Any other questions?"

"Can we use Mandy's camera to take pictures of the damaged school and post them on the Web site? Maybe you'll get more letters with checks in them."

"Now I know you belong in my family." His warm gaze heated to fire. "In case you missed it, I did just propose," he said.

"I want to say yes, but I always thought I'd marry a man who made at least fifty dollars a month," she said playfully.

"Ah, you want to know that I can support you." He held her at arm's length. "I have a nest egg . . . savings from past jobs and investments that I can't touch for a few years." He calculated in his head. "That could support the two of us living here in the style we've grown accustomed to."

"I have savings too, so that will help," Grace said.

"Are you sure, Grace? Can you really live in these conditions long-term?"

She looked skeptically up at him.

"You aren't having second thoughts?" he asked.

"I'm wondering whose bedroom we should move into," she said, snaking her arms around his waist, knowing she'd handle any conditions just to be at his side.

"Darling, I've imagined you in my bed every night since I saw you in that teddy. But I just want to marry you; I don't care which room we live in."

" 'Live'? I thought they were 'sleeping' quarters."

"Not anymore." His expression stirred her blood, reminding Grace of his arousing kisses.

She laughed. "Yes, I'm happy to marry you, Dr. Novak, the sexiest doctor in the world."

He lowered his head to kiss her. "You make me feel like the *luckiest* doctor in the world."

Their lips touched, and Grace thought she felt the earth move. She circled her arms around Ryan's neck, knowing her sensations had everything to do with the man kissing her and nothing to do with natural disasters.

The clinic door opened, pulling them reluctantly apart.

"Benita?" Grace said.

"Are you all right?" Dr. Novak asked.

"Yes. Sorry for interrupting," she said to them. "I have something for you." She passed an envelope to Grace.

"What is it?" Grace asked.

"An engagement gift," Benita said.

"But . . . how . . ." Grace stumbled over her thoughts.

"*El doctor* told me he planned to ask you to marry him. So I wanted you to have this."

Grace turned her puzzled glance from Benita to Ryan.

"Open it," he said. "I'm curious too."

Grace ripped the envelope and pulled out a photograph of the sexiest shirtless man she'd ever laid eyes on. *Wow!*

"Holy cow, Benita, this is the best present I've ever received!"

Ryan groaned. "Not that contest photo."

"Thank you. I'll treasure it forever," Grace said.

"Hey . . ." Ryan crossed his arms.

"You too. I'll treasure you forever too."

"*Mi novio . . . my sweetheart . . .* telephoned the cantina to see if I was safe," Benita said, smiling. "I told him the news of the baby, and he is driving down pronto, today."

"That's terrific!" Grace hugged her.

"I did not want him to find me with this photo."

"Everything will work out," Dr. Novak said, hugging both women. "The population growth in San Felipe is booming. The future looks bright."

"Dr. Novak, I think you've reached your goal," Grace said.

He gazed at her with a question in his eyes.

"The plaque you told me about. The one you saw every day and took inspiration from. The one that honored a doctor for his skills and compassion and that vowed he would never be forgotten."

"Darling, I did not dream of *reaching* that goal; I want to *live* it . . . with you." He bent and kissed her.

As her heart soared, Grace heard the clinic door close behind Benita.

Epilogue

Chad Novak had arrived in San Felipe to a fiesta in progress. The town square had been decorated with flowers and streamers. Even a yellow school bus had been adorned. The strains of mariachi music and voices and laughter floated from inside the church. He hadn't missed the wedding, had he? He hurried into the church.

"There he is!" Ryan said.

Everyone turned to look at him. A bride in white, a groom in a suit, his parents, the bride's family, and about a hundred other guests. Ryan rushed from the altar and embraced his brother.

"Did I miss the ceremony?"

"No, but since you're a couple of hours late, we got started on the reception."

Chad hugged him in relief. "Thanks." He glanced at the altar. "She's gorgeous. Just like you said."

The villagers gathered around them, wanting to be introduced to *el doctor's* brother. Grace made her way down too.

"I've heard so much about you. We're pleased you're here." She clasped his hand.

"I wouldn't miss my brother's wedding for anything. Except a broken propeller on an airplane." He kissed her cheek. "I appreciate your waiting for me."

"Is the best man ready?" a fully recovered Father Sanchez said to Chad.

"You bet."

It took a few minutes to quiet the guests down and get the bride and groom back to the altar. A pregnant woman waddled to her spot as the matron of honor.

The ceremony was a traditional Mexican wedding with candles and a rosary lasso. Chad got choked up once or twice. Not only from hearing the sacred vows exchanged, but also by the outpouring of love from the villagers for his brother and his new wife.

After the groom kissed the bride, pews were moved aside, cloth-draped tables were brought in, and the festive reception resumed. Then Chad's moment came to toast the newlyweds.

The music stopped, and everyone quieted. Chad lifted his glass of sangria.

"Congratulations to Ryan and Grace. Two special people who deserve all the happiness and love and good fortune in the world for the rest of their lives." He paused. "I never met Grace before today, but I knew she was the one for my brother when I saw her gift registry. Instead of china or silver, she asked for X-ray film and cartridges and oxygen-rebreather devices . . . you get the picture."

Everyone chuckled.

"There's one thing on the registry I was especially pleased to purchase." He glanced at his parents. They stood with a beautifully wrapped box. "It's a neonatal belt for listening to a fetal heartbeat. I see you have an immediate need for it. . . ."

All eyes and grinning faces turned to Benita and her new husband.

". . . but I hope you'll have a personal need to use it several times in the future."

Applause and whistles erupted from the guests.

"To the best brother in the world. I've always been proud of you, but never more than today. I love you." Chad's voice cracked. "And, dear Grace, welcome to the family."

More applause and happy tears followed. Then the music started again, and laughter and good wishes filled the church.

Chad marched through the happy crowd to his brother and handed him an envelope. "It's a receipt for the deposit wired to your San Felipe bank account this morning."

"I'll open this with Grace later. Is it close to what we hoped?"

"It exceeds what we hoped." Before Chad could tell his brother about his new idea, the families pulled the new couple out to the dance floor.